Look for the other books in the

DIADEM

Book of Magic

John Peel

AN
APPLE
PAPERBACK

SCHOLASTIC INC.
New York Toronto London Auckland Sydney

Cover art by Michael Evans

No part of this publication may be reproduced in whole or in part, or stored in a retrieval system, or transmitted in any form or by any means, electronic, mechanical, photocopying, recording, or otherwise, without written permission of the publisher. For information regarding permission, write to Scholastic Inc., 555 Broadway, New York, NY 10012.

ISBN 0-590-05949-1

12 11 10 9 8 7 6 5 4 3 2 1   7 8 9/9 0 1 2/0

Printed in the U.S.A.
First Scholastic printing, October 1997

This is for David Levithan
for all his contributions

PROLOGUE

Sarman sat upon his throne, brooding. Carved from a single immense diamond, the throne sparkled in the lights of the huge room. In front of the throne was a large, polished mirror, upon which flickered images that Sarman was only half watching. About the room, the Shadows writhed and shifted, waiting for orders from their master.

"They may be getting too good," Sarman mused, stroking his dark beard. He shook his head. "They are only children, though, and still new to magic. How good could they possibly be?"

"They will be no match for you, sire," the closest

Shadow whispered. "No one is, not even the Three Who Rule."

"The Three Who *Ruled*," corrected Sarman. "*I* am the One Who Rules now. Don't ever forget that." The Shadow whimpered and retreated, realizing it had made a potentially fatal mistake. Luckily for it, Sarman had other things to concentrate on.

In the mirror, he could see forms of the three people he was studying. "Score, Pixel, and Renald," he said softly. A street rat from Earth, a computer nerd from Calomir, and a girl warrior from Ordin who had begun by masquerading as a boy. Hardly the sort of people one would expect to become great magicians. And yet, these three were doing just that. They had defeated and killed that idiot magician Aranak. They had fought trolls and goblins, and then made friends with the same goblins and a handful of centaurs. That was unheard of in all the worlds!

Yes, these three were far more dangerous than he had anticipated. But they were also absolutely necessary to his plans. Sarman had seized power, but it was taking too much out of him to maintain it right now. He was a prisoner in his own fortress, chained to his own throne. There was just one way to free himself, and to roam the Diadem at large — his now by right of conquest!

He needed these three brats here, where he could kill them and absorb their power.

Right now, they had crossed over to Dondar, and that was a short journey away from the center of the Diadem, where he waited for them. He had to make absolutely certain that they came to him.

"Shadows!" he cried. "To me!"

There was a hissing, a bubbling, and then, as swiftly as they could, the Shadows seethed across the room to listen to his commands. He hated having to rely on them, because none of them were overly bright, but they were all he could use right now. For all of his power, Sarman was reduced to catching glimpses of the children in his mirror and having his dark agents spy on them and nudge them in the right direction.

"Go to Dondar," he ordered the Shadows. "Watch the three youngsters. Make certain they head for the gateway here. Don't interfere unless you have to, but they *must* come here! I need them." He lowered his voice and stared about the room at the Shadows. "If they don't get here, for any reason, then I am going to personally rip each and every one of you into tiny little shreds. And *then* I'll kill you. I'm sure you all understand me. Now, go! To work — and make certain those brats are here soon!"

The Shadows hissed their understanding of his orders, and then writhed away toward the gateway to Dondar. They would all do their best to see that his orders were carried out. Soon, hopefully very soon, the three children would be in his power. . . .

And then he could drain them and kill them, and he would be free once more. . . .

Not very long now . . .

PART 1

CHAPTER 1

"**N**ow, this is something," said Score, awed at the scenery before him. He and his companions had just stepped through the gateway from Rawn and emerged here on this new world, Dondar. Rawn had been very pretty, but, apart from its odd-colored trees, had looked very much like Earth. It had been almost easy to forget at times that they were on an alien world.

But Dondar was *very* different.

The sky was a faint purple, touched here and there by cotton-candy clouds. The grass was a rich blue color. The trees that he could see were all tall, thin and bent into strange shapes. Their leaves varied in shades of blue, purple and orange in a kaleidoscope of color. There was no way that he could think, even for a second, that this was Earth.

"I could almost get used to this," Pixel said, looking around admiringly. "It's really pleasant."

"And probably very dangerous," Helaine finished. "Everywhere we've gone so far has been. We'd better be prepared for trouble." Her eyes were scanning the horizon already.

"Lighten up a little," Score told her. "We've only just arrived. I'd say we have a good ten minutes before we're due to be attacked." He grinned to show he was joking. "Anyway, it's time to take stock, don't you think? We have to figure out what we're doing."

"We're following somebody else's plan, as usual," Helaine growled. "I know we chose to do it, but I don't feel comfortable with it. I'd sooner be in charge." That was true enough, Score knew: She was a warrior from a world where women were supposed to do as they were told. She'd pretended to be a boy named Renald until recently so that she could get away with her behavior.

"So would we all," Score agreed. "But we need more information. You know that. All we know for certain at the moment is that we're being drawn somewhere by some unknown enemy who controls the Shadows. That person doesn't want to kill us — at least, not yet — because the Shadows actually saved our lives once. And there's someone else involved, trying to help us, who's sending us cryptic messages and the Pages that we keep picking up and that still make very little sense."

Pixel nodded. "And don't forget the Three Who Rule. They're tyrants who control all of the worlds of the Diadem from their central world that only magicians can enter. Right now, we're on Dondar, one of the Inner Circuit worlds and just a jump away from their home base."

Helaine frowned. "If Shanara is correct," she added, "then we're being trained as weapons to fight the Three, because we have tremendously strong magical powers ourselves. And Oracle said that we will have to face the Three before our journey is over."

"If we can believe a word that he says," Score commented. "I still don't trust him."

"Neither do I," agreed Helaine. "But it is possible that he's trying to help us, as he claims. Even if he does talk in riddles and rhymes."

"I do what I must; I do what's allowed.
At least you'll admit, I stand out in a crowd."

Score spun around, and saw that Oracle had simply appeared, as he always did, without warning. He was dressed completely in black, as usual, with a slightly mocking smile on his face. They still didn't know much about him, except that he claimed he wasn't really real, and that he was trying to help them. On the other hand, Shanara had believed he worked for the Three Who Rule, which could make him an enemy agent. And he'd also cheerfully betrayed each of them at least once, while claiming it was for their own good. He claimed that he was forced by the spell that had created him to speak in rhymes all the time, and that he couldn't help giving them sometimes obscure comments instead of direct help.

Oddly enough, that made some sort of sense to Score. Though magic was everywhere in the Diadem, it was strongest closer to the center and weakest at the edges — where Earth was. Something had corrupted the magic, though, and from time to time it wouldn't work properly. They'd almost been killed several times when their magic had backfired without warning. If Oracle had been created by magic, then he was probably affected by this corruption, and unable to do what he was supposed to do.

"Now what do you want?" Score growled. Every time Oracle showed up, it usually meant trouble.

"Your decision was wise to continue your quest
For you have reached the ultimate test.

More Pages are here, more Pages abound
And you shall not rest until they are found."

"Well," Helaine commented, "*that's* a change. Good news for once." She turned to Pixel. "That's your job, I imagine. You have the ruby."

They had discovered that their magical abilities were intensified if they focused their minds through different gemstones. Each one had a different property, and the ruby enabled Pixel to locate the position of anything he might want. Thanks to the goblins on their last world, each of them now had four different gems. Helaine had the Book of Magic that explained how each jewel could be used.

Oracle held up a hand.

"Your quest will continue when you meet
   with a stranger;
But first there will be, as always,
   a danger. . . ."

And he vanished, like a TV being turned off.

Score groaned. "That we needed to hear?" He looked around, but everything seemed to be absolutely peaceful. "Do you think he was kidding us, just to get a rise out of us?"

"If we assume that, we'll be in big trouble," Helaine replied. She now held her sword at the ready, and was scanning the woods. "But I can't see any trouble at all."

"That's because you're looking in the wrong direction," Pixel said in a very nervous voice. "Something's casting a very large shadow, and I don't think it's a cloud."

Looking upward, Score almost screamed at what he saw. It was *huge*, something like forty feet long, with two huge wings beating slowly.

A dragon . . .

Its body was thick, with spines down its back like on a stegosaurus. Its long tail, held out straight as it flew, ended in a couple of long, nasty-looking spikes. Its long legs had large claws, and its elongated snout had a mouth packed with teeth. And it was swooping down toward them.

"Head for cover!" Helaine cried, sprinting toward the closest trees.

Score followed as fast as he could. Even Helaine wasn't crazy enough to suggest that they fight a beast like this! Her sword would barely scratch it, because the dragon's skin looked as if it were armor-plated.

It would be a close race, Score realized, as he

concentrated on running. But if they could make it to the trees, the dragon wouldn't be able to get at them so easily. It was too large to be able to follow them in, and some of the trees looked to be too tough even for a dragon to uproot.

Twin trails of fire screamed down from the sky ahead of them, setting the strange grass alight and shutting off their retreat.

Just what they didn't need . . . a fire-breathing dragon!

Score skidded to a halt. They couldn't go on, or they'd be cooked. But, right now, they were out in the open with no protection at all. And the dragon would be on them in seconds.

Which meant it was time to use magic again. He fished in his pocket for his emerald. This enabled him to transmute one thing into another. He'd used it against the goblins to dig pits for them by turning soil into air. Maybe it was a good time to reverse that concept. Trying to forget his fear and panic as the dragon drew closer, Score concentrated his mind on changing the air into something more solid. . . .

And a shield of rock sprang up out of the ground between them and the dragon.

"Nice one," gasped Pixel beside him, panting with the effort of their run. "That should —"

The dragon, screaming in fury, slammed into the rock wall. Under the tremendous impact, the shield simply broke apart, scattering rocks in all directions.

"— do nothing at all," Pixel finished, sounding really worried. "Time for plan B — if we have one."

Colliding with the wall had luckily slowed the dragon down. Huge eyes glaring down at them, it beat its wings and gave a couple of short bursts of fire from its mouth as it fought to stay aloft.

Pixel's eyes opened wide. "Of course! It's aerodynamically unstable!"

"What are you talking about?" snapped Helaine, her sword back in her hand again. Even if it was useless, she was going to go down fighting.

"The dragon," Pixel said excitedly. "It shouldn't be able to fly. It's heavier than air, and those wings aren't big enough to lift it. Besides, it only beats them very slowly."

Score didn't want an analysis of why a dragon shouldn't be able to fly when it obviously could. "It's magic, then," he yelled. "Who cares?"

"No," Pixel insisted. "It's a hot-air balloon! It's staying aloft because of its fire. I've seen balloons do that. They puff out a little fire to rise in the air."

Score nodded. "You may be right," he agreed. "But how does it help us?" He gestured at the dragon, which had now regained its balance and was starting to attack again. "And preferably help us fast?"

"We can start fires with our magic," Pixel pointed out. "Maybe we can snuff one out magically, too."

"It's worth a try," agreed Helaine. "Maybe if we all concentrate . . . ?"

Score wasn't sure he could focus on anything other than the huge creature hurtling down at them, teeth and talons ready to rip them all to shreds, but it might be their only chance. Feverishly, he pictured a fire in the belly of the dragon, burning brightly. That was what was keeping the dragon aloft. . . . Then he pictured the fire dwindling down to nothing, and finally vanishing in a puff of smoke. He concentrated hard on this image as the shadow of the dragon grew larger and larger. The spell for *creating* fire was *Kula shriker prior*, and he could only hope that saying it backward would put one out. "Roirp rekirhs aluk!" he howled, with only seconds to go before they were torn to pieces. . . .

"Move!" screamed Helaine, pushing both Score and Pixel. They both stumbled and then ran, Helaine keeping pace with them. Score glanced up at the dragon, now almost on top of them. . . .

It looked startled and suddenly very scared. It

tried coughing fire, but nothing happened except a small amount of smoke issuing from its throat. It had worked! They'd put out its fire!

But it was still going to hit where they had been standing. In panic, they ran as fast as they could from the spot, to avoid being crushed in the impact.

And then the ground shook as the dragon slammed into the earth at full speed, unable to stop itself. It was like being caught in a minor earthquake, and Score was thrown from his feet. He hit the ground, and his left side was a mass of pain.

But he was alive.

He looked up, and saw the vast bulk of the dragon only about twenty feet away. One of its legs looked as if it were broken, and the monster was definitely out cold. It was still breathing, though, its chest heaving and falling in long, slow gasps. They hadn't killed it, but it was certainly out of action for now.

Score sat up and gave a long sigh that turned into a yelp of pain. He must have bruised his ribs when he fell. It was a small price to pay, since he was still alive. "Well," he commented, "that was a bright stroke, Pixel. It worked."

The other boy grinned. "Sometimes I even amaze myself," he said. Score could hear the relief in his voice.

"You did well," Helaine commented, clambering

to her feet. "But we'd best be on our way before it wakes up again. I don't think it would be easy to fight on the ground."

Scrambling to his feet, Score nodded. "I'm with you there. Let's put as much distance from this barbecuing beast as possible."

They hurried away, casting anxious glances back over their shoulders as they did so. The dragon lay still, shaking only occasionally as it breathed.

"It'll probably be able to restart its flame when it wakes up," Pixel said. "I just hope we're well out of its sight by then. It isn't likely to be in a good mood."

"It might be an idea to decide which way we want to go," Score commented. "I mean, any direction away from that thing is fine, but maybe we're also heading away from any further Pages."

"A good point," agreed Pixel. He hefted the ruby again and stared into it. Score knew he was focusing his mind to search for any more of the mysterious Pages that might be on this world. A moment later, an intense beam of red light shone from the gemstone. It lit up the path ahead of them and slightly to the right. Unfortunately, the crystal distorted his speech so that it reversed the syllables in all he said. To understand him, the others had to switch the syllables back. "Well, we were inggo mostal in the right tiondirec," he commented. "There's otheran Page bouta tythir lesmi waya. I could feel it. But it's dedsurroun by gicma."

Score sighed. "It sounds like another magician has it. I wonder if this means trouble."

"It usually does," Helaine observed. "But we'd better head in that direction. It looks like a valley of some sort down there, with a river running through it. That'll mean water and fresh game, so we'll be able to eat well tonight, with luck."

"With your hunting skills, you mean," Pixel said with a grin. Score winced. He'd almost forgotten that Pixel seemed to be developing a crush on Helaine. It was a dumb idea, because any idiot could tell just from looking at her that she'd never be interested in romance. She was all business, and had virtually no gentler qualities whatsoever. Pixel was bound to be in for a rude awakening one day soon.

They came to the banks of the stream, which was only about ten feet wide, but quite deep. Helaine bent and scooped a little water in her hands, tasting it. "Delicious," she pronounced. "It's pure water, with a hint of orange in it. Now —" She broke off and stared downstream, her eyes narrowing.

Score turned to see what had caught her attention. More trouble? Then he stopped, astonished.

Three . . . creatures stood beside the stream, staring back at them. Each roughly the size of a small

14

horse, but much more delicately shaped. Long legs, a long neck, and a thick, bushy tail that flickered as they stood there. Tufts of hair almost covered their delicate hooves, which didn't look right somehow.

And in the center of their foreheads, each of the creatures had a long, delicate-looking spiral horn.

"Unicorns," breathed Helaine, entranced

CHAPTER 2

Helaine couldn't think straight as she stared at the three unicorns that were standing beside the stream, watching her back. As a child, she had loved nothing more than the stories about unicorns that her mother had told her. She had often dreamed of walking into a wood somewhere, and a unicorn would step out to greet her. . . . Helaine had always pictured a unicorn as being just like one of her father's war horses with a pointy horn stuck on. The reality was very different. These unicorns possessed grace that even the finest horse couldn't, and an overwhelming sense of power and personality.

And now, here she was — her fantasy becoming

real. She was about to be greeted by not one but three unicorns. The one in the center was clearly their leader. He was slightly taller, but radiated an air of control. His lithe body was mostly black, with splashes of white, spread like stars across his coat. To his left was a female, a reddish-pink in color, with touches of purple. To his right was a second female, slightly smaller than the first. She was primarily white, with flecks of gold. The horns of each of them were identical — about two feet long, spiraled and shining slightly like mother-of-pearl.

They were absolutely beautiful. Helaine had never seen anything like them. Even Score and Pixel appeared to have been struck speechless with awe, though Helaine wasn't really paying them any attention. She was focused on the three unicorns, who had come to greet her, as in her fantasies. It was amazing.

Then the male put down his head, aimed his horn at them and charged.

That broke the spell completely for Helaine. They weren't being *greeted* — they were being *attacked*. Helaine's first reaction was to move for her sword, but she hesitated. Even if this unicorn attacked her, she knew she'd never be able to harm it. The thought of using her sword on him made her almost physically sick. There had to be another way to handle this. . . . *Magic!* Of course. She had her powers, plus a handful of gems that would concentrate her abilities. Reaching into her pouch, she pulled out one of her four jewels, and took a quick glance at it. It was a brownish stone, and she recognized it as agate. The Book of Magic said that it was a communications gem, for telepathy. Its distortion was simple: Words would not be spoken aloud, only in the mind.

Well, now was the time to see if it worked.

The unicorn was running at her, the beautiful horn now a wicked weapon aimed at her chest. In a few seconds, she'd either have to move or be killed. Instead, she concentrated, and sent one telepathic word: *STOP!*

The black unicorn was so startled, he almost tripped over his own feet. But he swerved to one side and came to a halt. Astonished eyes met hers. *Was that *you*?* a voice asked in her mind.

So this worked both ways! *Yes, it was,* she thought. *What do you think you're doing?*

Defending my herd's grounds! came back the indignant reply, and she saw anger flash in his dark, deep eyes. *Against human predators!* Then he calmed down and stared at her again. *But none of them has ever *spoken* to one of us before.*

Score moved closer to her. "What's going on?" he demanded. "I can hear a voice in my head, and it must

18

be *him*." He pointed at the unicorn. "And I can hear you thinking at him, too."

Helaine held out her hand. *It's the agate,* she explained without audible words. *It creates telepathic communication.*

So that's it, the unicorn answered, snorting and shaking his mane. *It's a magical trick. I might have known! You can't trust a human!* He looked as if he were ready to attack again when the strawberry-colored female moved to block his path.

No, Thunder, she snapped. Helaine could clearly hear the anger in her voice. *I'm not sure that there's any need to hurt them.*

Thunder glared at her, and shook his head slightly. *Who is the leader of the herd?* he demanded. *Who guards the ways for it?*

But these humans aren't trying to harm us, the other unicorn objected. *They're *talking* to us. Behaving like intelligent creatures, instead of like humans for once. I think we should talk back. It's only polite.*

It's a trick, growled Thunder. *You can't *talk* to humans. They're all alike — greedy, savage and unprincipled.*

*We are *not*!* Helaine yelled back at him. *We've done nothing to hurt you. And we wouldn't ever hurt you.* She held up the agate. *You can read my thoughts because of this. Take a look, and see if we mean you any harm at all.*

When Thunder refused to budge, the red female moved forward and stared into Helaine's eyes. Helaine felt something like fingers tickling inside her brain, and she felt very peaceful and content. It was the female unicorn. Suddenly, she knew her name was Nova, and the other, more nervous female was Flame. Thunder was the herd's leader, and justifiably suspicious of humans. He was also rather self-righteous. In fact . . .

Helaine jerked her head back, and the feeling went away. She'd been reading Nova's mind in return! Those were Nova's feelings and memories she'd been seeing. It had been amazing. For a second, she had felt the joy of being able to gallop across a summer meadow, the breeze ruffling her mane, her cloven hooves dancing on the soft grass . . .

Nova turned back to Thunder. *She is telling the truth,* she said firmly. *These humans mean us no harm. They are travelers, and are being hunted.*

Then they are already bringing further humans after them, Thunder objected. *Humans are like fleas; they never come alone, and never wait for an invitation to set up home. Send them away.*

We can't send them away, Nova replied. *They're strangers here, and need our help.*

Help? Thunder stared at her in amazement. *Nova, the next thing you'll say is that you want to keep them as pets because they followed you home! Even if they don't directly mean us any harm, they're *humans*! They'll bring trouble upon us if they stay, you mark my words.*

The white unicorn, Flame, moved closer. Helaine could now see why she was more shy than the others. She was obviously younger than they were. In fact, she realized from Nova's memories, she was the daughter of Thunder and Nova. *Father,* Flame thought, *don't be such a grouch. They seem quite nice to me.*

*And what do *you* know?* asked Thunder. He sounded angry, but because of the agate, Helaine could tell he was only trying to protect his daughter. *You're only eight years old, and still wet behind the ears. Haven't I always told you that you should *never* trust a human?*

Yes, agreed Flame. *But you also told me to admit it when I make mistakes.* She moved forward, and stood in front of Helaine. Helaine smiled back at her, staring in wonder at the unicorn's gold-flecked eyes. She was simply the most beautiful creature Helaine had ever seen in her life.

Thank you, the unicorn replied. *And I like you, too.* She seemed to lower her voice somehow.

Don't listen to my father; he's always like that. But he's not really as bad as he sounds.

I am, too, Thunder snapped. *I still think we should kill these humans now, on general principle. You can't trust a human!*

You're prejudiced against humans, and you're not thinking straight, Nova said firmly. *You *know* they mean us no harm, and Flame likes them. What would be so bad about allowing them to travel through our lands?*

Never, replied Thunder. *You can't trust them, no matter what you think. We're not helping them at all. And we're not allowing them to cross the herd lands. They can just take the long way around.*

Through the dragon marshes? asked Flame, shocked. *Daddy, you *can't* make them do that. They'll be killed for sure!*

That's none of my business, Thunder replied. *And none of yours, either. If they're killed and eaten by dragons, it will serve them right.*

No! said Flame, very forcefully. *Daddy, I *like* this Helaine. I want to be friends with her.*

Friends? Thunder looked absolutely shocked. *That's impossible. They're not civilized. You can't trust humans!*

*You mean *you* can't,* said Nova primly. *Thunder, settle down and think for a moment or two. These humans have tremendous powers. They're three of the most powerful magicians I've ever encountered. They could kill us quite easily if that's what they wanted. But they've done nothing to harm us, and all they want to do is to cross our land. Maybe get a little food on the way. Where's the harm in that?*

If they were anything but humans, Thunder replied, *I'd agree wholeheartedly with you. But they *are* human, and you *know* what a treacherous, despicable breed they are. I'm not leaving any daughter of mine alone with a human. If they're going across our lands, then I'm coming along to watch them every inch of the way. I'm not going to let them out of my sight until they're gone. They're just the sort of danger I have to guard the herd against.*

"Fine,* said Nova. *That's a very sensible decision. Just what I'd expect from the herd leader.* She winked at Helaine. *You just have to know how to talk to him,* she said in a mental whisper that Thunder obviously didn't overhear. *Now he's guaranteed to look after you, even if he calls it keeping an eye on you for trouble.*

Helaine realized that the mother unicorn was obviously much practiced at handling her irritable husband. *Thank you,* she said simply. *My friends and I really appreciate your kind offer. We promise to do nothing to betray your trust in us.*

Thunder just snorted. *Well, let's get moving. If I've got to put up with you, let's make it as short a time as possible. Where are you heading?*

I'm not entirely sure, Pixel admitted. *We're looking for a way off this world.*

Well, that's the first bit of good news I've heard today, Thunder replied.

But before we can do that, we're after some magical Pages, Pixel continued. *They've been scattered for us, but the magic seems to have gone wrong, and they've fallen into the hands of other magicians. We believe the next Page is in the hands of someone ahead of us.* He pointed in the direction the ruby had indicated.

That figures, Thunder snapped. *The local wizard. I *told* you these three are bad news!*

What's the problem? asked Score, worried. *Is he or she a nasty person?*

We don't know, Nova replied. *He or she is human, and by Thunder's policy, we have nothing to do with humans. We've never seen or met the magician.*

But two of the herd have vanished without explanation, Thunder snapped. *And close to the magician's castle. I don't want to make it five.*

Then just tell us the way to go, Helaine said.

We don't want to get you into trouble. Then you can stay here and be safe.

No, Thunder answered. *You're not crossing our lands without an escort, and that's final. I'll take you as close as is safe. My wife and daughter can come part of the way, but no farther. And that's also final,* he added, before either female could get a word in. Neither of them answered him. Helaine wondered if that meant they'd do as he said — or whether they were just waiting until later to argue.

You're not really as obnoxious as you try to sound, are you? she asked him, wondering if she dared to reach out and stroke his sleek hide.

Yes, I am, he replied with dignity. *And if you so much as lay a hand on me, I'll bite it. Pick up your feet. Four, if you've got them; two if you don't. Let's get moving before I change my mind.*

Sarman, alone, stared into his seeing mirror. Those blasted brats had somehow made friends with unicorns! It was unheard of! Did they go around spreading happiness wherever they went? They were obviously either far more clever or far more stupid than he had given them credit for. He hadn't expected the three of them to be so adaptable when they'd been selected as his victims. All he'd specified was that they had to have magical abilities; the rest had been left to the Fates. Still, it really didn't matter in the end. He was bound to defeat them, no matter how powerful or clever they might be. For one thing, he was much more experienced than they were. He knew his abilities to the final fraction, whereas the three of them could barely remember any spells without the help of that book the girl had. For another, he had his weapons. And, finally, he knew his enemies — and they still didn't have a clue who they were fighting.

Crossing the room, he entered a smaller chamber off his throne room. The Shadows were never allowed in here. This was the heart of his power base, the reason why he was now ruling the Diadem.

In the center of the room was a vast, mobile tapestry of light. Dozens of different gemstones, each representing a single world in the Diadem, moved slowly above the floor in a huge, bright cartwheel. All but three of the worlds thus represented were glowing, pulsing with an inner light. Only the sapphire, the emerald and the ruby were dark and lifeless — the stones representing Earth, Ordin and Calomir. They were the last jewels that needed charging with lifeblood.

And, very soon, they would be charged, and his own Diadem would be completed. Then he would be able to relinquish this small suite of rooms and roam at large in the Diadem — which he would own and control. All he needed now to complete his grasp on power were the three children. . . .

A small table had been set up beside the door. On it rested three doll-like figures. Each was a perfect likeness of one of the three youngsters. Pinned to the dolls' chests were their true names: Matt for Score, Helaine for Renald, and Shalar for Pixel. Sarman had discovered these names with ridiculous ease. Now he had two elements he needed to control his foes: their image, in the form of the dolls, and their true names. All he needed now was the third element, substance.

And that was what the Shadows were seeking. A few drops of blood, five or six hairs, or even a nail clipping would be sufficient. With such items, Sarman could attune his images to the real people, and then the three of them would be within his power. Now that they were on the Inner Circuit, they were close enough. It was important that the chosen elements be freshly taken when he finally faced them.

And then he could kill them, and drain their life forces into the jewels in his own private Diadem. Since each child was a representative of their own worlds, that would then make his images into control focus points for the worlds. As he would be able to control the children with the dolls, he would be able to control the worlds through his jewels.

In a very short while, every world within the Diadem would be under his sway. Then he could restore the damaged magic, and rule the Diadem alone. Until his Diadem was complete, though, it was draining his power, and he could not leave this castle and world. And the poison spread magically throughout the Diadem was hurting him, too. He had to have his model complete to restore magic to its former effectiveness.

He *needed* Score, Helaine and Pixel.

Now!

CHAPTER 3

Pixel walked along feeling almost cheerful. Helaine and Flame seemed to be off in a private world of their own, chatting and laughing together. They had quite clearly bonded in some fashion, and he couldn't help smiling at them. They were so happy. It occurred to him that he'd never really seen Helaine laugh before, except in the face of danger. She didn't have much of a happy life.

And neither did Score. When the first burst of telepathy had struck them, Pixel had suddenly been able to take a brief glimpse into the minds of his companions. Even though the agate belonged to Helaine, the effects of it had encompassed them all. He wondered if they had felt the same thing with his mind. Score, he had seen, was maladjusted and antisocial because of his upbringing. His father had beaten Score and his mother, and Score's mother had died young. The poor guy had never really known love. With Helaine, it had been different. As a girl, she was considered by her father to be nice, but a burden. He wanted a son and heir, not a daughter, no matter how talented she was. A daughter's only worth was as a bargaining tool, to be wed to someone her father wanted allied to his cause. Her feelings were irrelevant. Faced with this chasm, Helaine had adopted her male disguise and striven to become a *somebody*. A person her strict father might note and admire. And it had almost worked for her. . . .

As for himself, Pixel shrugged mentally. He'd been lucky, really. His parents had never harmed him, nor had they demanded the impossible of him. They had simply cared for him and ignored him. Lost in their virtual worlds, they had left Pixel to his own devices. He was lucky. He hadn't been beaten or scorned. He'd just been left alone.

Had his parents even missed him yet? Pixel thought hard, and realized that he had absolutely no idea how long it had been since he'd last seen them in the flesh. The House had fed and clothed him. His parents only contacted him through E-mail if they wanted to check up on him. He hadn't physically seen them in . . . Well, he didn't know. Maybe two years. Maybe more.

He wondered if he should be missing them, but he wasn't. They'd been missing for far longer than he had. In fact, if it wasn't for his life being constantly threatened, he would be almost perfectly happy.

Nova moved next to him. *You seem preoccupied,* she thought at him. *Is it anything you'd care to share?*

Pixel shrugged. *I don't know if you'd even understand,* he admitted. *I was simply thinking that I'm almost enjoying myself. A nice walk, you guys to admire, friends with me . . .* He gestured at the landscape. *If it wasn't for constant danger, this place would be almost paradise.*

Thunder, a little way ahead, sniffed mentally. *There's no danger here,* he announced. *I keep the unicorn lands free of trouble. And it'll be free once again when you're gone, human.*

Pay no attention to him, Nova murmured. *He's just prejudiced. Still, humans have done some awful things to our kind.*

Yeah, Pixel said, not knowing really what she meant. But the creatures on all of the worlds he'd visited had had it in for humans. *I've been thinking about that, and I've an idea why. The only humans that can reach Dondar are magicians, right?*

Right, agreed Nova, clearly intrigued.

And to become a magician, you generally have to study real hard for years. And fight to get stronger and better. It's a sort of mind frame, where you have to take what you want. Magicians tend to become very selfish in that case, and out for more power.

Exactly, said Nova, nodding. *Magicians, on the whole, are a very self-centered and nasty lot.*

But we aren't like that, Score, Helaine and I, Pixel pointed out. *For some reason, we've got a lot of power, but we haven't had to steal or fight or cheat to get it. We just have it. And, honestly, we don't really want it. I'd be happy enough to be normal again. We've not learned to be selfish and greedy with our power. Quite the opposite.*

Nova studied him in amazement. *You know, I think you have something there,* she agreed. *You really don't desire power?*

Pixel shrugged. *What would I want power for?* he asked. *To rule a world? Why should I care about ruling anything? It doesn't interest me.*

It's easy to say that now, Thunder said ominously. *But when you get older, you'll become like all of the other humans, you mark my words. You're all alike.*

No, Pixel said firmly. *No, we're not. I don't want to be in power. I don't want to have slaves or servants, or even a castle of my own. It doesn't interest me.*

Thunder gave a whinny of disbelief. *Then what *does* interest you?* he challenged. *What do you aim to do with your life, human?*

Pixel hadn't really considered this. *I don't know,* he admitted. *I guess I've been concentrating most on what I *don't* want, not what I *do* want.* He thought for a moment. *I don't want to have to keep fighting for my life,* he said finally. *I don't want to be constantly on the run. And I don't want uppity unicorns telling me I'm a nasty, evil person.* That made Nova laugh, and Thunder simply snorted. *What do I want? You know, I've always wanted to make a difference. Not to be part of the crowd, but to do something good. And I think I could use my magic that way. To help people — and unicorns, and goblins, and whomever. I always felt so much a loner back home. Oh, I had friends, but they weren't real friends. And I mean that in every sense of the word *real*. They existed only in my computer world. I wasn't really with them, and even if I thought I was touching them, it was just an image.* He gestured toward Helaine and Score. *These two, however, are real friends. Oh, they can be real pains, too. Helaine is stuck-up and aggressive, and Score is often rude and obnoxious. But . . . I don't know. I *feel* for them, and I like them.*

Nova nuzzled him with her nose. *You seem like a nice person to me, Pixel,* she commented. *I hope you get through this trial you're facing all right. I think you may well yet make a difference to this world. And maybe others.*

He's a human, Thunder repeated. *He'll change. He'll get nasty, mean and selfish, just like the rest of them. You mark my words.*

Pixel grinned. *You said I'll *get* to be that way,* he pointed out. *That means that even you admit I'm not like that right now. So you should be nicer to me.*

Nova snickered at this. *He's caught you out there,* she thought gleefully to her husband. *Come on, admit that these three humans are decent folks. Even if you think they won't stay that way.*

Humans are like cockatrices, Thunder commented. *They hatch nicely, and they're cute when they're babies. And they're killers when they grow up. Rules of nature never change. Even if this human *wants* to be nice, his whole heritage is against him. He'll end up as bad as the rest of them. You —*

— mark my words, chorused Pixel and Nova together. Then they both broke down, laughing, as Thunder stormed off ahead of them indignantly. Pixel

stroked Nova's neck affectionately. *He's really not all that bad, is he?* he asked.

No. He just likes to sound very stern and strong. Nova laughed again. *He's afraid of looking like an old softie — which is what he really is. But it's not all put-on. He does have good cause to hate most humans.*

Why's that? asked Pixel interestedly.

At that moment, Helaine gave a start. *Trouble!* she exclaimed.

What? Nova whirled around, but neither she nor Pixel could see anything.

It's coming, insisted Helaine, drawing her sword.

There's nothing wrong, Thunder snapped, galloping back to be with them. And to stand between Flame and whatever might be wrong, Pixel noted.

Helaine can see trouble before it arrives, Pixel said. He had been intending to call her *Renald*, but since they were communicating telepathically, it wouldn't have worked. The unicorns would have read her real name anyway, and then been suspicious of him for giving her a false one.

*As I said earlier, there's no trouble on *my* lands,* Thunder growled. *I take good care of my herd.*

Then you're slipping up, Score answered. *Look!*

Pixel stared in horror at what was approaching them. It was over thirty feet tall, and clearly not a natural creature. It was made of solid rock — actually, solid *rocks*. He could see where boulders had somehow been persuaded to join together to form a vaguely human shape. The thing had two legs, two arms, and a semblance of a head, though without any features whatsoever. Pixel could fairly feel the magic of the thing.

It looks like the local magician isn't too happy to see us, he commented.

*I'm not too happy to see *that*,* answered Score, clearly as worried as Pixel. *It looks unstoppable to me.*

Thunder reared up, whinnying loudly. *That creature of magic doesn't belong on *my* land!* he yelled.

Yes, but attacking the creature with just your horn wouldn't be a smart move, Helaine snapped. *You'd just break it. I think you'd better let us handle this.*

Great idea, Score growled. *Any idea *how*? And you'd better make any suggestions fast. It's going to stomp us into the ground in about thirty seconds.*

The rock creature was advancing quickly on them. Thunder seemed to be undecided as to what to do. He really was indignant that this thing was on the unicorn range, but clearly saw Helaine's point that attacking it by himself wouldn't get him anywhere.

Magic, how else? snapped Helaine. *Let's focus on trying to levitate it. If it's not on the ground, it can't walk toward us.* She held her sapphire up in her hand and started to focus.

Pixel watched the approaching giant as she worked. He felt the magic reach out . . . But she simply couldn't summon enough mental energy to lift the thing.

"It's too heavy," Helaine gasped, sweating from the strain. "This isn't going to work! Let's scatter!" she exclaimed, pocketing her gem and diving to one side, Flame close behind her. Pixel went the opposite direction, Nova close by his side. Thunder and Score ran off together.

The stone giant paused, and stood, watching them for a moment. Even though it had no obvious eyes, it could clearly make out its intended victims. Now that they'd split up, who would it choose to go after first?

It turned to stride after him. Pixel sighed. Just his luck!

I hope you can do something, Nova said urgently. *Otherwise, we're in danger of being stomped flat.*

I'll try, Pixel replied. He fished in his pocket for one of his own gems, praying that whatever he drew out would be useful. Pulling out a jewel, he glanced down at it. It was a bright yellow in color, and sparkled in the sunlight. That reminded him that it gave him control over the element of fire. But rocks couldn't burn. That was useless!

Unless . . . He was already pretty good at throwing fireballs. Maybe, with the topaz to increase his power, he could throw something big and hot enough to do the trick? It was worth a try — especially since the rock monster was barely six of its paces away now.

Pixel concentrated on the topaz, and then twisted with his magic to start a fireball. Would this work? As he felt the magic within him, a basketball-sized spinning globe of fire was formed in the air about ten feet above him. It seemed to be so *small*, but then Pixel felt the heat the fireball was giving off. It was burning so hot, it was white instead of the usual red and yellow. Quickly, he magically threw the ball as hard as he could at the advancing rock monster.

The flames hit it in what would be its head. Pixel stared in mixed hope and fear as the flames burst over the creature. Was it strong enough a spell? He hardly dared breathe, focusing all of his power through the topaz, thinking only *burn . . . burn . . . burn.*

And the fire grew. It blazed out, white-hot and all-enveloping. Pixel gave a gasp of relief as he saw it was having the effect he had hoped.

The rock was melting, and dripping, then flowing. The heat of the fireball was turning the solid monster into a fountain of lava. Great, steaming globs of rock melted and ran down the creature's body, dripping to the ground, where the grass blazed into flames from the heat. The rock thing staggered to a halt, its head gone, its body now melting down into slag. The arms broke free, shattering in the air and collapsing to the ground. Lava hissed and bubbled as it fell to the ground. Seething molten rock flowed until the rock creature had utterly vanished, leaving only cooling lava and the brushfires that had been started.

The others all yelled out their relief, though Pixel couldn't make out their words at this distance. Even Thunder was prancing about, excited as a colt. He'd forgotten his dignity for the moment, and he actually looked happy for a change.

Pixel felt another wave of magic, and readied himself for another attack. Then he relaxed, realizing it was Score using a chrysolite. That jewel gave him power over water, and he had managed to create a small but powerful rain cloud over the burning grasses, and the steady downpour was dousing the flames. It was a smart idea.

Skirting the blackened stones and burnt grasses, Pixel and Nova rejoined their companions.

Way to go, Score said admiringly. *Good thinking.*

Helaine clapped her hand on his shoulder. *We'll make a warrior out of you yet,* she promised, smiling.

Thunder sniffed. *Not bad . . . for a human,* he commented. *Of course, you were just fighting against something created by another human without respect for our lands or lives.*

Grouch, muttered Flame, but with affection. *I am so amazed at what our new friends can do.*

They're no friends of mine, Thunder snapped. *They're trouble. You mark . . . You'd better believe it.* He tossed his head, his mane flaring in the air. *Well, that's enough of this. Let's get moving again. The sooner you're off our lands, the safer I'll feel.*

I'd like to be able to say the same thing, Score muttered. He glanced at the cooling rocks. *But I doubt that this was the last problem we'll face before we reach this magician.*

Helaine nodded. *If at first you don't succeed . . .* she quoted.

With that depressing thought in all of their minds, they moved out again. Helaine and Flame were together, though a lot more somberly this time. Score and Thunder seemed to be together, though neither

40

paid the other much mind. Nova fell in beside Pixel again.

You three have quite amazing abilities, she said. *We've seen and heard of other magicians before, but very rarely of one with powers like that. To melt that rock creature down took amazing power. You three truly are very special.*

That made Pixel feel uncomfortable. *It's not our fault,* he said, embarrassed. *We didn't ask for these abilities.*

It's a gift, the unicorn replied. *And a gift like that should be accepted and appreciated. Thunder thinks you'll use it for your own selfish purposes, but I don't think so. The three of you seem much too nice for that. And I speak with knowledge here. Our minds have all touched, and it wouldn't be easy for any of us to hide anything from one another.*

Pixel felt another flush of embarrassment. Did Helaine know that he liked her, then? If so, what would she do about it? This telepathy business might help in some ways, but it caused problems in others!

Perhaps you are those who have been spoken of, Nova mused.

Huh? That comment dragged Pixel back from his own thoughts. *What do you mean? Spoken of where? And by whom?*

Nova appeared to be gathering her thoughts.

Then she looked up at him. *There are certain prophe-
cies among the unicorns,* she explained. *Though we
do not exactly possess magic, we *do* have the next
best thing.*

And what's that?

She chewed at her lip, and then shook her head.
I'll leave that to Thunder to tell you — or not, she
replied. *It's one of our closest-guarded secrets. Anyway, let's just say that while we can't *do* magic, we
can have an effect *on* magic. As a result, humans seek
us out to be of use to them. Sometimes we are kept
alive. Usually,* she shuddered, *we are killed and
butchered. *That* is why we dislike and fear humans.*

Pixel was astonished. *Who could ever be so hor-
rible as to kill someone like you?* he asked. The
thought of even hurting a unicorn made him shake.
You're so noble, so beautiful . . .

I know, agreed Nova. It wasn't pride, simply
acknowledging a fact, as if he'd said: "The sun is shining." The unicorns knew and accepted what they
were. *But when humans are greedy for power, there
is very little limit to what they will do. Anyway, one of
our herd, many years ago, was captured by a magician
and used in some magic ritual. The magician wanted
to know the future, and she conjured up visions of
what was to come. The unicorn, Vixen, saw everything. At the end of the visions, the magician was so

shaken that she accidentally lowered her spells and Vixen managed to escape. She brought us the news of what she had seen. She had been driven out of her mind, and could hardly speak. But she said that there would come three strangers one day who would save the Diadem. We always assumed that she meant unicorns, but now I wonder if she meant humans *

Pixel wasn't sure what to make of this. A while ago, he'd have scoffed at the very idea of prophecy. Now he discovered that the idea didn't disturb him unduly. But what did it *mean*? Why weren't things ever *clear* in this whole business? They needed some time to sit down, relax and go over things. Maybe together they could work it all out. For all his annoying behavior Score was pretty bright. And Helaine was wonderful. She could do almost anything. Except keep her temper! Perhaps they'd get a chance when they stopped to rest to have a group discussion. Even the unicorns might be able to help. They seemed to be pretty smart.

Hold it, Score said from in the lead. *Come and look at this.*

Puzzled, Pixel and Nova sped up a little. They drew close to where the other four had gathered around an object in their path. It was a pyramid of some shining metallic substance, about four feet tall.

No unicorn made that, Thunder said with absolute conviction. *It's a human thing.*

A pyramid, agreed Pixel. *It must be meant for us. It's a triangular shape, and there's three of us. It *has* to be another message for us.*

Another Page, perhaps, agreed Helaine. *But how do we get into it?*

Perhaps we just pick it up, Score suggested. He leaned down and touched the pyramid — which threw off a large spark. Score recoiled.

Maybe not, Helaine observed sarcastically. The she stood back. A sign was slowly appearing over the pyramid. The numbers and symbols hung in the air like small clouds.

111 > 1+1+1

The power of the three combined is greater than the individual power of each of the three, Pixel stated.

But how does that help us? Score asked petulantly.

Pixel, Score, and Helaine looked at each other.

Then they realized the answer.

We have to do it together, they all thought at once.

Without a word, each of the three lifted a corner of the pyramid. It was seemingly weightless, lifting at their touch.

Beneath, there was another Page.

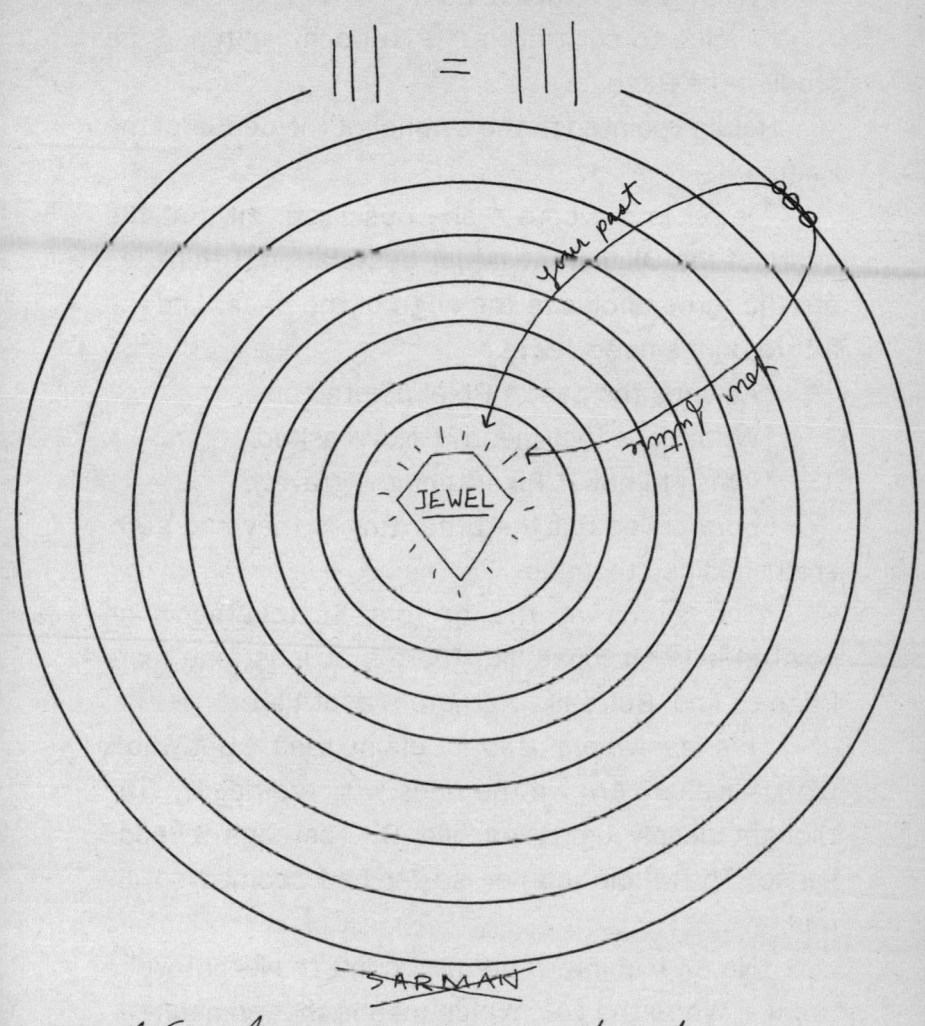

er. We fear we are dead.
e more. We await you.

What is it? Nova asked.

A clue to our travels, Pixel commented as he studied the Page.

Helaine pointed to the symbol at the center of the Page.

Jewel is the core, she observed. *It's at the heart of the Diadem. It is our destination. I think we are the three circles at the edge of the rings. And the future brings us to Jewel.*

As does the past, Pixel pointed out.

What does that mean? Nova asked.

I wish I knew, Pixel thought gravely.

Score pulled out the other Pages they had gathered and lined them up.

The words at the bottom fit together, he pointed out. *It looks like there's at least one more Page to find. But still . . . there's a lot here.*

We fear we are dead, Helaine read. *But who's we? Is we us? Are we the ones who are dead?* The thought deeply unsettled her. But perhaps it made sense. The whole journey so far had seemed so unreal. . . .

No, Pixel interrupted, *I don't think that we're the we. We're the you. Which means that someone — or something is awaiting us. Whatever it is.*

Sounds dangerous, Nova commented.

Thunder scoffed.

We must continue to move on, the unicorn leader announced. Pixel gathered all of the Pages for further study later on.

They left the trees, and found themselves on the banks of a river. It was about half a mile wide, and flowing quite swiftly. Pixel stopped dead and stared at it in dismay.

How are we ever going to get across that? he asked.

There's a ford about a mile upstream, Thunder answered. *We can cross it there.*

Good, muttered Score. *I've had my bath for this week already.* Pixel knew he was joking, though. Being with unicorns even seemed to have cheered up Score.

Helaine stopped still, and chopped the air with her hand. *This place stinks of magic,* she growled. *I can feel it — trouble.*

Heigh-ho, muttered Score. *Here we go again. What is it this time?*

Helaine shook her head, as if trying to clear it. *It's . . .* She gestured at the river. *That.*

Thunder scowled. *There's nothing wrong with the river,* he protested. *Good, clear, fresh water. There's . . .* His voice drained away, and Pixel could see why.

The water was churning now, not simply running.

It looked like a whirlpool was starting to form. So what? They didn't intend to cross here anyway, so who cared? But as he watched, the water began to bubble, then to fountain into the air. It looked as if something in the water was trying to emerge. But there was nothing there at all. Nothing but water.

Nothing but water. . . .

Pixel felt his skin crawl as the water started to take on a shape. It rose up, twenty feet into the air, churning and bubbling, but it didn't fall back. Instead, it stayed in the air, growing larger and stronger with each passing second. Twenty feet tall, the waterspout suddenly grew arms and legs, and the shape of a head.

It was just like the creature made from living rock. Only this one was made of pure water.

With a sudden lunge, it started to wade through the river, hands outstretched toward them all. . . .

CHAPTER 4

Score had no real idea what damage this creature made from living water might be able to do to them. Drown them, perhaps? But it was clearly not wading toward them to join them in a picnic.

Try that fire trick again, he suggested to Pixel.

The other boy nodded, and gripped his topaz. Score had to admire how good Pixel was getting with this magic business. The fireball formed immediately, and shot straight for the water thing —

— which simply split in two, and avoided the fireball. It roared right through where the creature had been a moment earlier, without causing it any damage whatsoever.

Uh-oh, muttered Score. *Not a good sign.*

Pixel braced himself, and willed the fireball out of existence before it could do any damage. Then he formed and launched a new one, at the chest of the water giant. Once again, the water simply parted, and the fireball passed harmlessly through. Pixel made the fireball evaporate. *This isn't going to work, folks,* he announced, worry very pronounced in his voice.

Then let's try something else, Score said. He clutched his chrysolite gem, and concentrated on the thing. This should give him power over water, and the thing was made from water. Therefore he should be able to control it.

But, concentrate as he might, he couldn't get a grip on the thing. It was exactly like it had been greased somehow, and he couldn't grab it. *It's not working,* he gasped. *I think the first spell on it is preventing me from enchanting it as well. I guess only one spell per monster is the rule here.*

Thunder nickered nervously. *It's almost ashore,* he pointed out. *And angry. I think it might be a good time to retreat. If I charged it, my horn would do no damage.*

Good idea, Score agreed. He turned and ran for the trees again. Maybe they would slow the water giant down. The others followed suit, and they all headed for the cover of the woods. Once they were in about ten feet, Score whirled around to see how this was affecting the water monster.

It had stopped right by the first trees, and for a moment Score felt a surge of hope that they had managed to elude it. Then the giant seemed to surge, and grow in size. Its chest expanded, and then burst into a huge wave.

Oh, great! It was going to try to flush them out. . . .

Score yelled as the wave slammed him from his feet and against the nearest tree trunk. It knocked the breath out of his lungs, and he started to choke as water filled his mouth. Then, thankfully, the flood was gone, and he gasped and hacked to regain his breath. His lungs felt as if they were on fire, and his back hurt in several places from where he had struck the tree. Helaine and Pixel looked equally waterlogged and pained. The three unicorns, being four-footed, had managed to stand their ground when the wave had struck, but they were all drenched and far from happy.

The giant had lost a little size, and was only about fifteen feet tall now. Score had a momentary hope that this meant it wouldn't be able to do that wave trick again many more times. Then he saw the snake-like thread of water that was lurching over the grass from the river. It struck the giant's ankle, and then the giant started to absorb the stream, growing again.

Terrific, Score muttered. *He gets a free refill with every purchase.*

Helaine staggered over to him, eyes hooded. *It's going to strike again in a minute,* she said. *If it keeps this up, we'll either be drowned or washed out to it.*

I'm open to suggestions, Score replied. *I can't think of anything at all that might work. I'd try transforming it from water into gas or something, using my emerald. But magic won't directly affect it. We need something indirect.*

It's an elemental, Pixel commented, joining them. *It's a personification of Water, like the rock thing was a personification of Earth.*

And Fire beat Earth, muttered Score. *But not Water. So what beats Water?*

Helaine's eyes sparkled. *Earth,* she said. She pulled a gem from her pocket, an apple-green colored stone. *And chrysoprase controls Earth.* She grinned as she concentrated on the gem.

Score watched the water giant. It had absorbed the snake-like stream, and was now just over twenty feet tall again. It was getting ready to surge and release another flood at them. . . .

And then the earth around it seemed to erupt.

Huge mounds of soil flew into the air, directed at the creature. It was as if some unseen construction equipment were tearing up the ground and throwing it at the water giant. The giant, startled, tried to split to avoid the soil, but this time the attempt didn't work. There was just too much soil, erupting from all around it. The soil slammed into the creature, and immodiately started to turn into mud.

"Now," Helaine yelled to Pixel. "Use your fireball on it. I've made it a creature of living mud. Bake it hard!"

With a whoop of excitement, Pixel blasted a fresh fireball at the muddy, dripping giant. It exploded like a second sun, and Score went blind for a second. When his eyes cleared, though, he could see the giant standing exactly where it had been, frozen in shape.

Helaine's plan had worked. The soil had turned the water beast into mud, and then Pixel's sunburst had baked it hard. "Way to go!" Score said admiringly.

The unicorns moved back to join the three humans. Even they looked impressed.

"I think I'm really starting to get the hang of this magic," Helaine said happily. "It's mostly a matter of making use of the right tools. Just like fighting, only the weapons are magical, rather than steel or wood."

The three of you seem to be a good team, Flame commented with admiration. *That's two monsters you've defeated that we could never have dealt with.*

Score shrugged modestly. *It's just a gift we've got. I'll tell you one thing, though. Doing all this magic has made me hungry.*

Nova laughed. *It's obviously hard work. Well, there's a nice spot to eat right on the other side of the river. We'll take you there. It's time for a break.*

If our unseen foe will give us time for one, Pixel pointed out. They walked back past the now-solidified giant apprehensively. He eyed the river. *Do you think he's going to try that again?*

No, Score replied, thinking about it. *If we're tired from fighting this wizard's creature, then he or she must be even more tired after creating and animating it. I imagine he'll have to rest for a bit, too.*

I agree, thought Helaine. *Besides, he or she didn't repeat the rock monster. Once we've figured out how to stop them, there's really not much point in trying the same thing again, is there? I think we should be safe for a while.*

Thunder led them to the ford he'd mentioned. Here there were large stepping-stones set into the water, each of them about four feet apart. The water bubbled merrily past them, leaving their upper surfaces perfectly dry. Score hopped along after Thunder, who leaped gracefully from stone to stone. In a few moments, they were all safely on the other side of the river. Thunder then led them to a shaded grove of trees.

Plenty for all here, he announced, gesturing with his horn.

It had to be some sort of unicorn garden spot, Score realized. There were several dozen fruit trees, all heavy with pear-shaped delights in bright yellow and indigo. Lower down were bramble-like bushes bulging with berries. The unicorns started to munch on mouthfuls of these. Score picked a small clump of them and took a tentative bite.

His mouth was filled with a moist, sweet taste, a bit like a pineapple. It was delicious and refreshing. Finishing his handful of fruit, he plucked one of the pear-like things next and tried again. Again, it was moist, sweet and heavenly. A bit like a banana and a bit like cherry. And altogether wonderful.

They all ate quietly and happily for about fifteen minutes. Score was stuffed, then, and retreated to the river to wash the juices off his hands and mouth. He then took a drink of water, changing it to cola as it entered his mouth. A perfect ending to a lovely meal.

The others, one by one, joined him beside the river to wash and drink. Score absentmindedly took off his shoes and socks and padded into the cold, clear water. *It's really nice here,* he told Thunder. *I can see why you like these lands so much. And why you want to keep them like this forever.*

For a human, the unicorn replied, *you're almost intelligent.*

Score wasn't bothered; he hadn't exactly been expecting a kind reply. But he didn't care. As they started off again, he fell in beside Thunder once more. He nodded at Helaine, who was walking with Flame, both of them obviously deep in conversation. *It looks like your kid doesn't share your prejudices about humans.*

She's young, Thunder replied. *She'll learn better as she grows older. She's only as mature as you are right now, so she's plenty of growing still to do.*

It was another of his insults, but Score refused to let it bother him. *What amazes me,* he said, *is the effect Flame's having on Helaine. I was starting to think that nothing would ever make her happy. I mean, we're talking a real rain-cloud personality here. But now look at her. She seems almost . . . likable.*

Thunder snorted. *There's a saying amongst us unicorns,* he offered. *No human is complete until they've met a unicorn.* He glanced oddly at Score. *It's a very old saying. And it's obviously no longer true. Most humans these days just want to kill or exploit us.*

Huh. Score grinned back at him. *But it means

that, once upon a time at least, unicorns and humans must have been friends.* He stared at Flame thoughtfully. *Maybe it's true the other way around, too. Maybe no unicorn is complete without a human.*

Whinnying in contempt, Thunder shook his head. *Once we meet humans, we're always left incomplete," he snapped. *Humans don't want *unicorns*. They want only our horns.*

Puzzled, Score stared at him. *Whatever for? I mean, it's lovely and all that, but it would make a lousy lamp stand. Or candlestick. It's better to leave it where it is, if you ask me.*

Thunder managed to look surprised. *You mean you don't know why humans want our horns?*

No. Should I? Score shrugged. *I keep telling you, we don't much care for the other humans we've met on our journey so far. Except for Shanara. She was pretty decent when she calmed down. The rest have been real problems.* He glanced at the unicorn. *So, what's with the horn-collecting business?*

Thunder's lips curled, and he shook his head. *No. If you honestly don't know, then I see no reason to tell you.*

Suit yourself, Score replied. *I could care less anyway.*

Heads up, Helaine called. *I think our unfriendly neighborhood magician's had enough rest.*

Score sighed aloud. "So, what's it going to be this time?"

"Since we've had creatures of Earth and Water," Pixel answered, "I'd suggest it's likely to be either Air or Fire next."

"Wonderful." Score rattled his jewels together in his pocket. "And if our experience so far is anything to go by, we've used Fire and Earth to fight them off. That means we'll need either Water or Air next, right? I've got the chrysolite for Water. So who's got Air?"

"Me," answered Pixel, drawing out a blue-green beryl. "So we'd best be in the front, I think."

Here it comes, breathed Helaine, gesturing through the trees.

At first Score couldn't make it out. Then he saw what had caught her attention: smoke rising in several spots. "I guess it's Fire," he said cheerfully. "That must be my field. After all, Water should put out Fire, right?" He held up his gem and waited.

Through a gap in the trees, they finally saw it. It was a towering, vaguely man-shaped flame, burning yellow-hot. It strode toward them, arms ready to reach out and grab them. Every time its foot touched the ground, the grass caught fire. It left burning fires in its footsteps. And if it brushed against a tree or shrub, it ignited in a quick, hot flame. Thunder snorted in disgust at what the fire creature was doing to his land. Score realized he'd better whip up a rain-storm once this was over to put out all of the smaller fires before they spread.

Then he concentrated on his chrysolite, staring into the olive-green stone and focusing his thoughts. Almost immediately, a large dark cloud formed over the flame being's head, and Score willed it into action. Rain began to descend like a waterfall onto the monster. Score grinned, expecting a fast end to this creature.

Then his grin was wiped from his face. The flame creature brightened to almost white-hot. Instead of the water falling on it and extinguishing the creature, the flames were causing the water to turn to steam and sizzle helplessly away!

Well, time to intensify his efforts! Score focused, and concentrated harder. The cloud grew into a thick thundercloud, and then lightning zagged down from it, striking the flame creature full on.

The flames increased in size and intensity. . . .

"Way to go," Helaine yelled over the rolling sound of thunder. "I think you're increasing its power, you idiot!"

I'm trying my best, Score answered grouchily. He switched to telepathy because of the noise. He was starting to get a little worried. Even the torrential downpour from his thundercloud was having no effect on the flame beast. All of the rain sizzled off as steam. *It's got to work. It's got to. Nothing else will.*

The flame being drew closer and closer to them, and Score was on the verge of panicking. He was hitting it with everything he had, and the monster was still coming. And this was one they couldn't dodge by hiding in the trees. It would just start a forest fire to get them that way. But he couldn't give up. He couldn't! Sweat streamed down his face, and he didn't even feel the rain slamming around him as the storm he controlled drew closer. All he could focus on was stopping the fire monster. And he was failing.

It's not Water that stops this one! Pixel suddenly announced. *It's Air.* He held up his beryl. *Knock it off now, Score. I'll handle it.* He'd obviously been struck by inspiration. Score didn't know what it might be, but he might as well do as he was told. His efforts were having no success, anyway. He willed the storm to cease.

The flame creature was only about twenty feet from them now. It bent slightly, reaching forward with one long arm made of fire. Score was sweating again, from the heat and from simple fear. If Pixel were wrong, they were going to become barbecue of the day. . . .

Then the monster hesitated, its flames shaking. It seemed to grow a little smaller, and Score realized this with a thrill. As he watched, the flames dwindled and then shrank to nothing, the fire monster vanishing into a puff of smoke.

He stared at Pixel in astonishment. "Okay," he finally said. "I give up. How did you do that?"

"Simplo," Pixel said with a laugh. "Fire burns because it has oxygen from the atmosphere to feed the flames. So I simply changed all the oxygen around it into carbon dioxide. Flames can't burn in carbon dioxide, and it simply extinguished itself."

Helaine laughed, too. "Brilliant!" she said in admiration. "I could kiss you."

"I don't think he'd object," said Score dryly.

Helaine blushed. "It's just an expression," she snapped. "I didn't really mean it."

Score snorted. If she hadn't meant it, why had she blushed like that? Was she starting to get soft on Pixel, too? Or was she just feeling good because the last monster had been defeated? Ah, well, who cared? As long as she didn't start getting mushy on *him*, she could feel whatever she liked for Pixel. Anyway, he had work to do. "I hope nobody minds traveling in a shower for a while," he said. "But I've got to put out the fires that thing started." He concentrated on his gem, and created several light clouds that sent a sheen of rain down all around them. It wasn't too strong, but it was sufficient to make the burning footsteps finally fizzle to nothing.

They started off again while it was still gently raining. Score grinned at Thunder. *Is it much farther to this wizard's lands?* he asked. *I mean, is there time for any more trouble?*

With humans, Thunder said darkly, *there's always time for more trouble. But we should be there in less than an hour. With any luck, the wizard will be too tired after that effort to attack you again in that time.*

Don't hope too much, muttered Score. *Our luck's been pretty bad so far, and I don't expect it'll get a whole lot better as the day goes on.*

It didn't. About forty minutes later, Helaine called out a warning again. Score and the others tensed themselves.

If the pattern keeps up, Pixel announced, *the next creature should be made from Air. And you, Score, should be able to stop it with Water.*

Score nodded, clutching his jewel carefully. *But if it's made of Air, how can it hurt us?* he asked. *I mean, we need air to live, and it's not exactly a problem.*

Nova shivered. *Maybe as a strong wind?* she suggested. *Or solidified in some way?*

No, Helaine said, a catch in her voice. *Nothing like that. Look!* She gestured through the trees ahead of them.

A thick, sickly yellow cloud was rolling along the ground. Tendrils snaked out, writhing like living things ahead of it. Wherever it passed, the grass withered and died on contact. Plants wilted, and the trees shed their leaves.

"Oh, great," Pixel said, terrified. "It's not literally Air itself. It's simply one element of it. I'd say it's a cloud of chlorine gas."

"And that's not good news, right?" asked Score, watching it poison wherever it passed. He wished he knew his chemistry better.

"No, it isn't," Pixel agreed, shaking. "It's highly toxic. If that stuff gets into our lungs, it'll burn them up. We'll be dead in seconds."

CHAPTER 5

Helaine stared at the creeping cloud of gas in alarm. It looked like it was moving slowly, but she realized that this wasn't the case. It was actually traveling much faster than they could run, and it was getting closer every second. She turned to Flame.

Maybe you and your parents should run for it, she suggested. *You could probably get away from it because you're so fast. Besides, it's really after us, so it probably wouldn't even chase you.*

I'm not leaving you, Flame said firmly. There was obviously no arguing with her. Helaine had come to realize that once a unicorn had made up its mind, there was no changing it. They could be very stubborn.

Then you'd better hope we can stop it some-how, Helaine said. She took a mental inventory of the gems she possessed and their powers. Sapphire . . . levitation. But the cloud was already floating, and she didn't see that the gem would help. Agate, for communication. The cloud wasn't alive, just animated by a magician, so that was out. Chrysoprase, which controlled Earth. But her last trick of showering Earth on the monster wouldn't work here — the gas would simply seep through any obstacle. Finally, amethyst, which changed the size of something. Maybe she could shrink the cloud until it was too small to harm them?

It was worth a try. Gripping the purple jewel, she reached out with her mind. And, like Score before her, discovered that she couldn't get a grip on the object. It was just like he'd said — there was already magic on it, and she couldn't affect it directly with her own magic. She'd have to use her magic on something else, and then get that object to affect the cloud. But none of her abilities seemed to be of any use here. Despite all her magical power, she felt so helpless.

Then Score gave one of his wicked grins, and held up his chrysolite. The power over Water? How would that help?

Unless . . .

Score conjured up a large cloud over the creeping

gas, and started it raining heavily on the foul yellow gas. Helaine grinned, too, as she saw the cloud hissing and vanishing.

Chlorine dissolves in water!

In moments, the disgusting cloud had vanished, leaving only a small pond where it once had been. The grass touched by this pond was withered and yellow, but the gas monster was now harmless.

"That was almost too easy," Score said, preening himself. "This enemy magician isn't that great, if you ask me."

"Don't get overconfident," Helaine warned him. "Whoever we're fighting has a lot of power." She smiled, though, to show she was actually quite proud of him. "Well, shall we continue? We must be almost there by now."

They set off again as before, skirting the edge of the lethal pond. Already it was starting to seep into the earth, where it would be harmless. Thunder gave it a filthy look for polluting his meadows, but didn't get too close to it.

It's only about twenty minutes to the edge of the wizard's land, Flame said. *Then what will you do?*

Try and see him or her, Helaine replied. *Maybe we can make them see sense, and get through the next bit without a fight. If not . . .* She shrugged. *I guess we'll do what we have to. I'm going to miss you, Flame.* She stroked her friend's mane. *You make me happy.*

Flame snorted. *Am I going somewhere?* she asked. *I'm staying with you. You may need my help.*

This isn't your fight, Helaine said, alarmed.

*I'm your friend," Flame answered. *I'm not going to abandon you when you walk into trouble.*

It's too dangerous, Helaine insisted. *And, besides, your father would never allow it.*

The unicorn's eyes twinkled. *You think not?* she asked. *Haven't you noticed that he's stopped complaining about you? That's quite amazing in itself. But he seems to almost like Score. He's staying close to the boy instead of patrolling on ahead, as before.* She laughed. *I told you, he's not really as bad as he tries to sound.*

Helaine saw that Flame was correct. Though Score wasn't talking to the black unicorn, they were walking closely together. And Nova stuck close to Pixel. Frowning, Helaine asked, *Is there something about unicorns and people? Some kind of bond or something?*

Perhaps, Flame admitted. *I must confess, from the second I saw you, I knew we were going to be friends. I can't explain it, and I don't care. I think the same is true of my parents and your friends. Perhaps unicorns and people really do need one another to be complete.*

Helaine stroked Flame's neck. *I know that it makes me happy to be with you,* she admitted. *This is something we'll have to try and figure out when everything else is over. If it ever *is* over. I'm beginning to wonder if there will ever be an end to our problems.*

Well, here's the start of the end, at least, Flame told her, gesturing ahead of them with her horn. Through a gap in the trees, Helaine saw a valley between two large hills. *That's the start of the wizard's kingdom. The castle is just beyond that valley.*

And our wizard must still be recovering from the power drain of that last attack, Helaine said, satisfied. *Maybe he'll be too weak to fight us when we arrive. Though I'm not going to count on it.*

This is the end of the herd lands, Thunder announced a few moments later.

Score gave him an odd look. *Then I guess you'll be going back now, then? You've done what you promised, and seen us off your lands.* He didn't sound too eager to be rid of the black unicorn.

Huh! Thunder snorted. *As if I'd trust you to not come right back onto our lands again the second my back was turned. I know what you humans are like, you mark my words. No, I'm going to come with you until you leave this planet. It's the only way I can be certain we're rid of you and your contamination.*

See, Flame whispered to Helaine, with a laugh. *I *told* you he'd help — and that he'd try and make it sound like he wasn't!*

Helaine thought it was amusing, too. Thunder, his dignity intact, led the way into the valley, his head held high as if challenging anyone to say anything at all. Nova gave a distinct snicker, but nobody spoke a word to Thunder.

The pathway was easy going, and after about fifteen minutes they came to a bend in the valley. As they rounded it, Helaine saw their target ahead of them.

This looked like a *real* castle! For the first time since she had left her home, she felt like she was on familiar ground. There was a moat, and thick stone walls. In the center of these walls was the castle proper, a large, sturdy tower some four stories tall. There was nobody in sight, and the drawbridge was raised. Visitors were not welcome, obviously.

What was the owner like? Well, they would soon know.

"Curse them!" snarled Garonath, turning away from the window in anger. "Blast them all into tiny little bits! They've managed to make it all the way here, despite everything I've done to stop them!"

"They're more powerful than you thought, aren't they?" came a thin, reedy voice.

Garonath whirled around, which wasn't easy, considering how immensely fat he was. He was a man who indulged all of his appetites, especially that for food. He wore a simple robe, loosely tied about his ample waist. His fat cheeks shook as he peered around. "Who's there?" he demanded, readying a spell. "Show yourself!"

There was a movement in the shadows, and then one Shadow detached itself, growing and getting closer. "It's me," the Shadow hissed. "There's lots more of us here to help you."

"Help me?" Garonath scowled. "What makes you think I need any help?"

A long, shadowy claw gestured toward the window. "The fact that they've survived everything that you've thrown at them. You're a powerful wizard, Garonath, but you're not very bright. Or adaptable. Nobody's ever beaten your army of monsters before, so you don't have a clue what to do next. But I do, and I'll be happy to tell you what it is. For a price."

Garonath considered. Like all the inhabitants of the Diadem, he had heard of the Shadows and their mysterious master. They had powers, he knew, and could draw on the power of their master when needed. And while the Shadow had insulted him, Garonath had

70

to admit that there was a measure of truth in what the wretched creature had said. He *was* stuck for ideas on how to handle these three brats. He'd grown lazy over the years, since nobody had ever before managed to defeat him, the Wizard of Forms. "What's the price?" he asked finally.

The Shadow told him.

Staring up at the drawbridge, Helaine couldn't help smiling. *There's a spell on it,* she said, feeling the magic from where she stood. *So we can't use our powers to open it directly.*

So what do we do? asked Score. *Knock? Fly over the walls?*

"Unicorns can't fly,* Thunder said hastily. *You're thinking of Pegasus.*

He gets airsick, Nova explained, ignoring the sour look her husband gave her.

No problem, Helaine answered. *We only need a little magic here.* Using her sapphire, she levitated herself and flew over the moat and into the gatehouse. It was almost exactly like her father's castle. She simply found the release lever for the drawbridge and tripped it.

With a hollow clanking sound, the capstan started to turn, paying out the chain that lowered the drawbridge. Helaine paused to ensure that the portcullis was firmly locked in place — she didn't want it to come crashing down on anyone passing underneath! — and then she levitated herself down into the courtyard to wait for her companions.

The castle was apparently deserted, but tidy. It seemed like such a waste to Helaine. A place like this should be filled with life, laughter and unicorns. Maybe, when all of this was finished . . .

Cool, Score commented, looking around. *Just like one of those British castles they use in fantasy movies.*

Helaine, as usual, had no idea what he was talking about. But she felt oddly pleased that he seemed to like this place, too. Maybe he did have some taste, after all. Helaine gestured at the main body of the castle. *The wizard's going to be in there,* she explained. *He or she will have rooms in that section.*

Why do wizards always have castles or palaces, and then have nobody to share it with? asked Pixel, taking out his ruby. *It's such a waste.*

"Because it suits me," said a thick, unpleasant voice. "And if something suits me, then I do it."

Helaine whirled around, her hand on her sword hilt. Standing between them and the drawbridge was one of the fattest men she had ever seen in her life. He had to weigh over four hundred pounds. Even his fingers were thick and pudgy, and he had several double chins. Fat seemed to be almost oozing from him. He had wisps of hair on the top of his head, and dark, brooding eyes. "And you are . . . ?" she asked.

"I am Garonath, Wizard of Forms. Don't bother to introduce yourselves — I already know who you are. And what you want." From the sleeve of his robe, he pulled a sheet of paper. "You're after this."

"Right," agreed Helaine. "We're willing to trade for it. Plus a way off this world, when we choose to take it."

"I imagine you could manage that?" asked Pixel.

"Of course." Garonath studied them for a moment. "You don't look like you have enough power to have survived my attacks."

Score grinned. "You don't look like you have the power to attack anything. Haven't you ever heard about exercise being good for you?"

Garonath sniffed. "I have magic, and that's very good for me. But not necessarily for you."

Thunder whinnied. *You've attacked them four times, and lost each time,* he sneered. *Do you seriously believe you will win now?*

Garonath's eyes widened. If he'd weighed any less, he might even have jumped. As it was, it took him a minute to regain his voice. "You can *talk*?" he squeaked.

*We've *always* been able to talk,* Thunder snapped. *It's simply that you humans never *listen*.*

This seemed to rock the magician's senses for a few moments. Pixel said helpfully, "We're doing it through telepathy; the unicorns aren't actually speaking. You're just able to pick up their thoughts, if they're directed at you."

"Really?" Garonath rubbed his flabby chin. "Well, it makes absolutely no difference in the long run. If you want to trade for this sheet of nonsense paper and a gateway to take you farther, there is a price."

Score nodded. "That figures. And what *is* the price?"

The wizard's greedy eyes fell on the unicorns. "A unicorn's horn," he said.

"No deal." Helaine felt a deep anger and contempt for this sick and self-indulgent wizard. "I have no idea why you'd even want one of their horns, but I do know you'd have to kill them to take it."

"You're being greedy!" Garonath whined. "You've got three unicorns. You can't possibly need them all. I only want one." He gestured at Flame. "The littlest one, even. Then I'll give you what you want — and more, if you like."

Helaine's anger was growing. "What part of *no* don't you understand?" she demanded. "These unicorns aren't our property, they're our friends, and we will do nothing to hurt them. Or allow them to be hurt."

Garonath's face changed from petulance to rage. "That does it!" he screamed. "I'm through trying to be nice. If you won't trade me a unicorn, I'll *take* one!" He muttered something under his breath, and a disembodiod hand the size of a cow appeared, floating in the air. It darted toward Flame.

But Helaine was quicker. She'd been expecting treachery, and focused through her chrysoprase, using her power over Earth. A wall of soil shot up from the ground, solidifying into iron in front of the hand. As it paused, she whipped out her sword, whirled it and plunged it through the hand, pinning it to the ground. It struggled feebly, but couldn't get free.

"Enough!" Garonath howled. With a gesture, he conjured up a huge whirlwind that howled about the castle's grounds.

Helaine realized that this was a ruse. Behind her, she could hear the drawbridge chain start to clank. Garonath had been hoping the sound of the wind would drown it out. Turning to Flame, Helaine ordered, *Get out now, all of you! He's sealing the castle magically! If you don't escape, you'll be trapped!*

But what about you? Flame asked, tortured by concern.

We can handle this! Helaine knew that was not

necessarily true, but she *had* to get the unicorns out before they were trapped. *Go!*

Thunder whinnied some sort of command, and the three unicorns whirled around and galloped for the rising drawbridge. For a second, Helaine didn't think that they would make it, but in a thunder of hooves, they charged to the top and hurled themselves across the gap in the moat. As the drawbridge slammed shut, Helaine caught a brief glimpse of the unicorns hurtling down the road away from the castle. At least *they* were safe!

It was a pity she couldn't say the same about herself, Score and Pixel . . . The wind was battering at them, and she lost her footing. She couldn't think straight, and she fell heavily, only to be battered along like a ball by the wind.

"You've ruined everything!" Garonath howled, like a child throwing a tantrum. "But I'll fix you! You just wait and see!"

Helaine saw that Score and Pixel were also being driven by the howling wind. They were all being bowled toward a doorway. She could feel the magical seal about the castle, one that they wouldn't be able to break. Perhaps Garonath wasn't the brightest magician in the worlds, but he was certainly pretty powerful when he wanted to be.

And then she saw the Shadows.

She knew that they were the agents of their unknown foe. On Rawn, they had attacked trolls to save the trio's lives. Now, on Dondar, they were almost solid, shapes of writhing blackness that pounced from the sky. On each Circuit, they became more solid. And more powerful.

Helaine was unable to escape from them. She couldn't even stand up, much less get out of their way. The black shapes descended onto her, and she felt their claws snatching at her, binding her and enveloping her. There was a twinge in her mind as the Shadows ripped her crystals from her pouch, leaving her without their aid. Her bow and arrows were likewise taken from her, and even the knife in her boot. Her sword was still embedded in the twitching hand.

She was defenseless now, and enveloped by the Shadows. They held her tightly, snickering softly to themselves. The wind died down, and Helaine's head finally stopped spinning. She could see that Pixel and Score were similarly wrapped inside cocoons of living Shadows. They were all completely trapped and helpless.

CHAPTER 6

Pixel couldn't act. He could barely breathe, because the Shadows enveloped him so tightly. And it was difficult to think. One thing was very clear, however: All three of them were now prisoners. Without their gems, their powers couldn't be focused properly. His had been taken, and he was certain that Score's and Helaine's had been, too, leaving them almost defenseless.

But only almost, because they could still perform magic. Just not as strongly. This didn't cheer Pixel too much. They hadn't been able to defeat Garonath *with* their crystals; without them, how would they even stand a chance?

The Shadows lifted him from the ground and drifted with him inside the castle. It was lavishly decorated, with huge tapestries on the walls. There were several large tables, and far too much furniture for one man. There were statues on pedestals, paintings on stands and trunks overflowing with jewelry. Since Garonath wore none of it, Pixel realized that the tubby magician had the treasure only because he wanted it. Unlike both Aranak's and Shanara's studies, there were virtually no books here; just a small case with about twenty slim volumes. Garonath was obviously not a big reader. It also explained why most of his spells were repetitious. He didn't know too many. Still, if the ones he did know worked so well, he probably didn't need more.

Puffing a bit from all his effort, Garonath followed his captives inside. He muttered another spell, and suddenly the Shadows released Pixel. Before he could either fall or stand on his wobbly legs, however, there was something new around him, holding him in place against one bare section of the wall. Score was positioned to his left, and Helaine to his right. Pixel realized that he was encased in a cocoon of dried, hardened mud, pinned by it to the wall. He could breathe, but couldn't move his hands and feet. The mud, thankfully, stopped at his shoulders, so his head was free.

"Like it?" asked Garonath smugly. "I got the idea from you. Don't try struggling," he added to Helaine, who was almost red in the face from her efforts. "You won't get free."

The Shadows darted back and forth in the air over their heads. "We have done as we have promised," one of them hissed. "Now it is time for our reward."

"Of course," agreed Garonath. He gestured at the captives. "Go ahead."

For one terrible second, Pixel thought that the Shadows were going to kill them all. They hurtled down from the air, hissing and screeching, their dark claws extended. But instead of ripping at his face with them, the claws settled in his hair. There was a slight pain, and then he saw the Shadow leap from him, clutching a lock of his hair. Two more followed the first, each carrying a clipping of hair from his companions.

"That's it?" Score asked, obviously relieved. "What is it, they're into collecting hair?"

Garonath ignored him for a moment. He turned to face the Shadows. "That's it," he said. "The price we agreed on for your help — fresh clippings of their hair. They're mine now."

"For the time being," agreed the Shadows, circling over his head. "But remember — Sarman wants them in one piece. But it doesn't have to be *very* alive. . . ." With a raucous laugh, the Shadow spun about in the air and vanished. Its companions whirled around, and they, too disappeared.

"Cheerful, aren't they?" asked Pixel. "So, would you care to explain what that was all about?"

Garonath ignored him for a second, and then shrugged. "Why not?" he decided. "It's amusing. You know that to control anything, you need three things: name, form and substance?"

Pixel suddenly realized what was going on. The name of Sarman had appeared on their Pages, another clue. "This Sarman has our names. He's made forms of us — some sort of dolls, I'd guess — and he wanted the hair clippings to add to the dolls. That's our substance. He's trying to control us."

"You're quick," Garonath said, impressed. "That's exactly his idea. Of course, it depends on your being alive when he's finished doing his spells. And I really don't have any reason to keep you alive. You've really irritated me. I've been after a unicorn for almost a century now, and I've never been able to get one. And today I had *three* in my castle. But, thanks to you, they escaped. And that really irritates me. So I'm going to get my revenge by killing you."

"Uh . . . won't that annoy Sarman?" asked Pixel hastily. "I mean, you'll mess up his plans."

"Tough."

Helaine snorted. "He's on the next world in the Diadem, isn't he?" she said. "The central world, Jewel." Like Pixel, she'd obviously realized that this was the world's name from the Pages.

"So?" Garonath's eyes were hooded, his expression unreadable.

"So he's obviously a lot more powerful than you are," she said. "And it doesn't strike me that annoying him would be the best way to stay alive for very much longer."

Garonath laughed at her. "You three really don't have a clue, do you?" he asked. "You're so dumb, I'm amazed you can even find your noses to blow them." Pixel felt a surge of hope. Helaine's comment had amused the magician, and he was talking instead of killing them. If only it could hold up . . .

But then what? How could they get free?

"You've heard of the Three Who Rule, I assume," Garonath asked.

"Yes," Score agreed. "They're the tyrants who run the Diadem their way."

Some of this was beginning to make sense to Pixel. The various Pages that they had collected and some of the cryptic clues they kept finding started to come together. "Sarman has defeated the Three Who Rule," he said, knowing he was right. "That's what we've been trying to figure out. He's defeated them and taken their place."

"Correct," Garonath agreed. "They're now dead. But Sarman doesn't have their power."

"If he doesn't have their power, how could he have defeated them?" asked Pixel.

"You're so naive," Garonath said, exasperated. "Partly by cheating. He attacked them when they were at their weakest."

"Of course," Pixel said, as it all started to fall into place. "The Three only had their proper power when they worked together. And in the past couple of hundred years, they haven't been getting along with each other very well. So Sarman stepped in and destroyed them, assuming the power over the Diadem himself. Right?"

"Pretty good," conceded Garonath.

"And for some reason," Pixel continued, "he's stuck on Jewel right now."

"Exactly." Garonath looked smug. "If he came here, he could probably destroy me, true enough. But — he can't come here! That's why he uses those creepy Shadow things to do his work. And they don't scare me. So, even if I destroy you and ruin his plans, there's nothing he can do about it."

"Are you *certain* of that?" asked Pixel, trying to worry the wizard.

It looked like he'd succeeded, too. Garonath stopped, a thoughtful look on his face. "I'm almost certain," he finally snapped.

"Almost?" echoed Score, derisively. "That could get you killed. Do you think he'd let you know *everything* he was capable of?"

It was a good point, and it struck home, because Garonath looked rather worried. Then his anger took control of him again. "No!" he howled. "You robbed me of my unicorns, and you have to pay for it! I'm going to kill all of you, see if I don't."

Pixel realized that, though Garonath was very powerful magically, he was mentally like a two year old. He was howling and crying for something he wanted, and when he didn't get all his own way, he would sulk or lash out. There had to be some way to stop him. . . .

And, suddenly, Oracle was there. He appeared out of nowhere, flickering in that slightly unreal way of his. Garonath jumped, and then scowled at the new-comer.

"Who are you?" he demanded. "Why are you here? Speak, before I destroy you."

"Over me you have no power
Even in this evil hour."

"We'll see about that," muttered Garonath. He said something under his breath, and then hurled a firebolt at Oracle.

It passed completely through the smiling man. Its only effect was to make him shimmer slightly more. He inclined his head.

"You cannot harm me, as I said,
For I am here only in your head.
The only way to get rid of me
Is to lose your head completely."

Even though he was a prisoner, Pixel couldn't help grinning at the terrible joke. So, as he had suspected, Oracle was some kind of magical projection, not a real person. But who had sent him — and why? Was he really their friend, or working for their unseen foe? If Shanara had been correct, Oracle had once worked for the Three Who Rule. If they were destroyed, was he now working for Sarman? Or was he trying to get revenge on the wizard who had killed his employers?

Oracle gestured to Pixel and the others.

"You must set your prisoners free.
To your salvation they are the key.

To Jewel now they must pass on
Or else the Diadem will be gone."

"Liar!" screamed Garonath. "You're just trying to trick me. They're just three helpless brats, and they've annoyed me." His face suddenly acquired a cunning expression. "If I can't hurt you, then you can't hurt me, either. You're nothing but illusions and hot air."

"Your words are true, I must confess
I could hardly hurt you less.
But by my warning you must heed
And not attempt this foolish deed."

"Oh, button it," snapped Garonath, confident now he knew that Oracle could do no more than talk. He turned back to Pixel, Helaine and Score, his face twisted by a nasty sneer. "This is one of your tricks, obviously," he said. "This must be one of your creations, a stupid attempt to sidetrack me. Well, it won't work. You're going to die." Concentrating, he began to mutter an incantation.

Pixel tried to concentrate. Okay, he couldn't use the crystals that had been taken from them, but that didn't mean he was powerless. The three of them all had the ability to perform magic, even without the crystals. He focused his thoughts on the table behind Garonath. It held all kinds of magical instruments, from crystal balls to tubes and jars filled with odd shapes in dark preservative liquids. All he had to do was to nudge them with his mind, make them fall from the table and distract Garonath. Or, better still, throw the jars at him.

But he couldn't do it. Pixel couldn't understand why at first, and then it slowly dawned on him. The mud that surrounded him was somehow dampening his magical abilities. There was a very strong spell on it that was somehow confining Pixel's magic.

Nothing he could do was going to penetrate that shield. . . .

He started to sweat, realizing that Garonath was actually a lot more powerful than they had imagined. Because he acted so childishly, Pixel had assumed Garonath had the abilities of a child. But that clearly wasn't the case. He was very powerful indeed, and he had them trapped.

Then Pixel realized that the magical dampening field would act both ways. It would prevent Garonath from hurtling any magic spell at them, too. So he'd have to lower the dampening field before he could try and kill them. And when he did that, Pixel had to be ready with his own magical response. He focused his mind on the table. As soon as the dampening field lowered, he was going to pick up the whole table and hurl it at Garonath. That should stop him long enough for them to break free. . . .

And then Garonath went to the table first and picked up a long, slender knife. With shock, Pixel realized that he'd underestimated Garonath again. The magician wasn't going to use magic to kill them. He was going to do it with a simple dagger.

And the dampening field wouldn't stop that, since it wasn't magical . . .

Pixel struggled again to get free, but couldn't move his muscles more than an inch or so in the dried mud. Garonath saw his struggles and laughed.

"That's right, you fool," he gloated. "Flail all you like. It won't get you anywhere. You're trapped and helpless, and nothing can save you now. . . ." Raising the dagger, he moved toward Pixel.

Pixel swallowed, unable to take his eyes off the glittering blade that was moving toward him. In seconds, it was going to rip into his flesh, killing him, and there was nothing he could do to stop it. This was the end, after everything they had been through. . . . The last thing he was going to see was the upraised knife and the insane gleam in Garonath's crazed eyes.

And then the door exploded inward, shattering into splinters under the force of some immense impact.

Garonath whirled around, shocked and startled. Pixel's eyes opened wide at what he saw there.

Thunder moved through the doorway, his eyes dark and angry, his horn lowered and pointed at Garonath. Behind him came Flame and Nova, and then five other unicorns, all glaring at the uneasy magician.

You wanted a unicorn, Thunder snapped mentally. *Well, then, take your pick. Which of us do you prefer?* He moved closer, and Pixel realized that the spiral horn on Thunder's head was glowing slightly. The mother-of-pearl look it normally held was gone, and it seemed to be glowing with some inner, ferocious light.

"Stay back," Garonath said, licking his lips. He was sweating now, though Pixel couldn't understand why. "I'll kill you if you don't."

Try it, Nova replied, her own horn lowered and glowing. She moved to Garonath's left, Flame following. Slowly, steadily, the other unicorns moved forward also, their horns low and gleaming with inner fire. *You know very well that magic won't work against us.*

"What are you talking about?" Helaine called. "Get out of here before he hurts you."

You don't understand, Thunder answered. *Why do you think Garonath wanted a unicorn's horn? Because it can negate magic, when used the right way.

The horn has to be prepared properly, which is what took us so long to get back.*

"Of course!" breathed Pixel, finally understanding. "Like gems! Your horn is some kind of channel for magic. That's why humans seek unicorn horns so much."

Yes, Nova agreed. *With a unicorn horn, you can defend yourself against any magic sent against you. A wizard who has a unicorn horn is impervious to magical attack.*

"Stay away," Garonath threatened, gesturing with the dagger he held. Thunder snorted, and flicked his horn. It sent the dagger spinning across the room, clattering into a corner. "I'm warning you!" Garonath screamed.

The time is past for warnings, Thunder replied. *It's time for action.*

The unicorns now stood in a complete circle around Garonath. At a signal from Thunder, they began to close the circle inward, getting closer and closer to the squirming, panicking magician. He tried to cast a spell, but it fizzled under the onslaught of eight unicorn horns. As Thunder had said, they canceled out Garonath's power entirely.

Which meant . . . Pixel used his mind, and exploded the mud that imprisoned him. He collapsed forward slightly, his legs unsteady after being imprisoned for so long. Helaine and Score followed his lead, and they stood together, watching what the unicorns were doing.

You wanted a single horn, breathed Thunder angrily. *Now you have eight of them . . .* His horn glowed even brighter, and then Garonath screamed.

Even at this distance, Pixel could feel the effects of the horns. They were stripping Garonath's power away from him, layer by layer. All of his magic was evaporating under the onslaught.

Garonath fell to his knees, whimpering, his hands outstretched, begging for something. Then Pixel saw that the hands were losing their layers of fat, too. They were becoming bony, and wrinkled and dark with age. With shock, he saw that the rest of Garonath's bloated body was becoming the same way. The flesh seemed to evaporate, and he became skeletally thin, barely dark skin over brittle bones. His few strands of hair turned gray, then white, and then fell to the floor like leaves in autumn. With a croak, Garonath started to collapse forward, a final sigh escaping his withered lips.

His body never hit the floor. It seemed to crumble, then become thin dust that floated away.

Pixel was shaking. He swallowed, and then stepped forward hesitantly. "Did you kill him?" he asked.

No, replied Nova, the glow in her horn dying down. She shook her head. *We simply negated his magic. He was almost a thousand years old, kept young only by his spells. He should have died centuries ago, and without his magic, that's just what he did.*

The other unicorns straightened up, the fires in their horns dying down. Most of them walked to the shattered door and went out, leaving only Nova, Thunder and Flame.

"Thank you," Pixel said humbly. "You saved our lives."

We couldn't let him hurt you, Flame answered. *Especially since you defended us at the risk of your own lives.*

"Some defense," Score commented. "You didn't need our help at all."

Actually, we did, Nova replied. *It's not easy for us to use our negation powers. We have to prepare for it. When we entered the castle, we were vulnerable. How else do you think humans can capture and kill unicorns? It takes a lot out of us to do what we just did. But you saved our lives, and we had to help you in return.*

And so, Thunder said darkly, *you now know our secret. With a unicorn horn, you, too, can become invulnerable to magic. If you were to kill one of us and take a horn from us, you would become safe from your mysterious foe.*

Pixel stared at him in horror. "Don't be crazy!" he exclaimed. "We couldn't hurt one of you!"

Not even to save your own lives? asked Thunder. He snorted. *You humans are all alike. Maybe *you* couldn't do it. But *she* could. Or *him*.* He nodded at Helaine and Score.

Helaine glared back at him. "I could never harm a unicorn," she replied haughtily. "Especially not Flame. It's unthinkable."

And you, street rat? Thunder asked Score.

Score scowled, and stuck his hands in his pockets. "You're a royal pain, you know that?" he asked. "But I wouldn't kill you for it. There are some things more important than safety. Like your friends. I won't deny I'd like to be protected from all magic, but if the price is to kill a unicorn . . . Well, I'm not willing to pay that price. No deal."

Flame laughed. *See?* she snorted at her father. *I *told* you it wouldn't make any difference to them. They're our *friends*.* She giggled. *You mark my words!*

Thunder had the grace to look embarrassed — which was not an easy thing for a unicorn to accomplish. *Well, I still think you can't trust any humans,* he snapped. *With *maybe* three exceptions, all right?*

"There's just one thing I don't understand," Pixel said, frowning.

Only one? asked Nova, teasing.

"Well, one major one right now. How come we could all hear your thoughts when Garonath had a dampening spell on us? We weren't in contact with the crystals — we still aren't, in fact. So how can we still hear you?"

Thunder coughed mentally. *It would seem that unicorns and humans can communicate by telepathy anytime,* he admitted. *It doesn't take magic to do it after all.* He shook his head. *We just didn't realize it at first, because it's been so long since there were humans worth talking to.*

"Right," Pixel said, "I think it's time to get busy." He crossed to the table, and picked up his gemstones. Slipping them into his pockets, he then snatched up the sheet of paper that Garonath had been taunting them with. "The next clue," he said.

"Great," said Score, reading it over his shoulder. "Well, some of that makes sense, at least. The bit at the top has to be the crown that we already figured out. And it looks like a reflection of it, too."

"But what about the other bits?" asked Helaine.

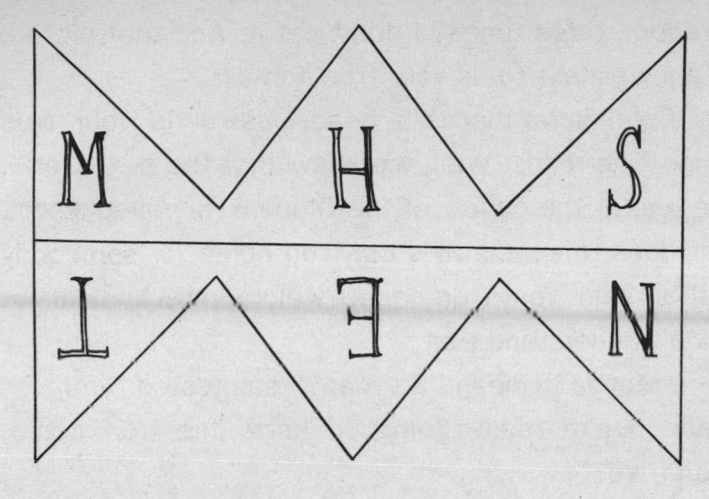

reborn   reborn   reborn

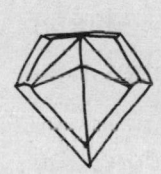 IS YOUR   YOUR
TRUE HOME
NAMES
WE → WILL
SOON
BE
→ KNOWN

u are the only hope. You m
ou do not stop him, the Dia

"*Reborn*, three times? I don't get it. And that picture of a jewel next to 'is your true home'?"

Pixel scratched his head. "Jewel is your true home," he read. "Well, we know that the next world, the one at the center of the Diadem, is called Jewel. But does this mean it's *our* true home, or somebody else's? And 'Your true names will soon be known' . . . I don't understand that."

"Maybe it means Sarman?" suggested Score. "I mean, we're really going to know his true name, aren't we?"

"It says *names*," Pixel pointed out. "Anyway, let's forget that for a moment. We've now got six Pages. There's writing along the bottom of them all. If we put them together, maybe we can make a message out." They fished out the other five Pages, and laid them with the sixth on the table. Pixel shifted them around until they could read the completed message:

"*The Diadem has been corrupted at the core. You are the only hope. You meet the future with the past. We are banished from the center. We fear we are dead. The treachery of Sarman has taken over. If you do not stop him, the Diadem will fall. Come to us. In magic, we became children once more. We await you.*"

"Well," Score said eventually, "that still doesn't make a whole lot of sense. Whoever sent this thing to us thinks they're dead — and they're *still* waiting for us? I don't know about you guys, but that news doesn't exactly make me feel a whole lot happier."

CHAPTER 7

"Well," said Pixel, "at least things are starting to make more sense now. Thanks to the Pages we know that our mysterious foe is Sarman, and that he's attacked and defeated the Triad, establishing himself as ruler of Jewel. And that it's his seizure of power that's somehow corrupted the magic all around us, causing it to fail from time to time."

"Yes," agreed Helaine. "But we still don't know so much. Why are *we* important? Just because we've got this built-in talent for magic? Or for some other reason? And what is *he* up to?" She gestured at Oracle, who had been standing silent, watching what was going on. "Who sent you?" she demanded. "Why are you here? And what happens next?"

Oracle came back to life with his usual slight grin.

"On to Jewel you must travel.
There your fate will true unravel."

"To *Jewel*?" asked Score, horrified. "Now wait a minute! That's where Sarman rules. The dude with the ultimate power. The guy who took out the Triad. And you expect the three of us to go there and confront him? No way. I'd sooner stay here and cut my own throat. It would be quicker and less painful."

Helaine shook her head. "Score's being a little melodramatic," she said. "But he's got a point there. If this Sarman can defeat the Triad, what chance do we stand against him?"

Oracle sighed.

"Your illusions I'm afraid I'll shatter.
You have no choice left in this matter.
Sarman all along has schemed
To use you to achieve his dreams.
He will not allow you to retreat
For without you he will face defeat."

"Great," muttered Score. "So he's not going to let us go anyway. Whatever happens, we have to face him."

"Wait a minute," Pixel said as something occurred to him. He stared at Oracle. "You said that we'd have to face the Triad before this was all over. But according to Garonath, the Triad is dead and defeated. So you *are* lying to us."

"Yeah!" Score agreed, staring suspiciously at Oracle. "I never did trust you, you phony. You've been lying to us all along, haven't you?"

"The truth I've told you every time.
Though constrained to speak in rhyme.
The Triad, too, you must yet face
Before you can achieve your place.
Though Sarman has defeated them
To life they seek return again."

"Time out," Score snapped. "This is getting *seriously* weird here. You're trying to tell us the same thing as the Pages? That though they're dead, they can somehow come back to life? That we've got to face ghosts?"

"Not as ghost or spook or ghoul
Entreat you to this timeless duel."

100

Score shook his head. "Thanks for nothing," he said. He turned to Helaine and Pixel. "Look, talking to him is getting us nowhere. It really doesn't matter if he's on our side or not, since he's just telling us stuff that makes no sense. We have to decide right now what we're going to do next. That's the important thing."

Pixel sighed. "It sounds like there isn't much we *can* do," he said. "According to Oracle, Sarman's going to come after us because he needs us for his plan. I think that much at least is the truth. After all, the Shadows have been driving us toward this point all along. Aranak and Garonath tried to kill us despite the Shadows and their warnings. And the Shadows even saved our lives once.

"Added to that, the Shadows have taken clippings of our hair. Garonath said it was because Sarman is making effigies of us so that he can control us. He knows our form, and he has our substance. He may be able to compel us to come to him whether we want to go or not."

"But he doesn't have our true names," Helaine objected. "That's how we managed to defeat Aranak."

"Sarman is much more powerful than Aranak," Pixel pointed out. "I'm afraid it's possible that he might indeed know our true names."

Score growled. "So what you're basically saying is that he's going to defeat us," he said. "He has all the weapons, and we have nothing."

"It does look that way," agreed Pixel despondently. "If only we had some way of fighting back. But we don't know his true name — I'm sure Sarman isn't it, if Garonath knew him by that name. And we don't know what he looks like. And we don't have any of his substance. So we have no control over him."

"Is that supposed to cheer me up?" asked Score. He collapsed into a chair. "So — we're doomed, then?"

No, Thunder said abruptly. Score stared at him, and the unicorn leader squirmed slightly. *Look, for humans, you three are pretty decent. I'd . . .* The words seemed to choke within him, but then he managed to say them. *I was wrong about you. You're almost nice enough to be unicorns. There is one thing that would help you: a unicorn horn.*

"But we already told you," Score answered. "We won't hurt one of you for a horn. That's out of the question."

Which is why we're giving you this, said Thunder. He gestured to the doorway. One of the other unicorns entered the room, carrying a horn in his mouth. *One of our number was killed several months ago by a dragon. We were too late to save her life. But we re-covered her horn.* The unicorn lowered the horn into Helaine's hands. *We now pass it along to you. It has been properly prepared. Use it wisely.*

Helaine had tears in her eyes, and even Score had a lump in his throat. "You're trusting us with this?" she asked, a catch in her voice.

We wouldn't give it to anyone else, Flame told her. *Normally, no non-unicorn is entrusted with a horn. But we know that you three need it, and will use it properly. We trust you.*

Helaine threw her arms around Flame's neck. "Thank you."

Score smiled. "It's nice to have a weapon at last," he said.

*It's not *that* powerful,* Thunder cautioned him. *You have to use it as a focus, like you do with a gem. But it won't stop all magic against you. It will, how-ever, weaken it. But don't think it's invincible. That's a good way to get killed.*

"I understand," Helaine replied, sliding it into her bag. Then she removed her Book of Magic. "This was what I dreamed about," she said softly, opening it. The label, *Property of Eremin*, caught her eye again. "I wonder who Eremin is — or was?" She started to flick through the pages. "Maybe there are some spells in here that can help us. If Oracle is right, then we're going to be in trouble soon."

"How much more trouble can we get into?" asked Score. "Anyway, we can't go anywhere. The only place to go from here is Jewel, at the center of the Diadem. But we don't know how to open a gateway, and Garonath's in no shape to do it. So we're stuck here for now."

"It won't last," said Pixel firmly. "I can feel it. Something is going to happen very shortly. We're almost at the end of our quest." He glanced at the Book of Magic. "Your dream came true, Helaine," he mused. "Maybe ours will, too. I can still see that huge wheel of gemstones spinning around. I just wish I knew what it means."

"Yeah," Score agreed. "And that dream I had was about a tune. I could whistle it in my sleep — if I weren't tone-deaf. Helaine's dream came true really early on, but nothing like our dreams have turned up. Yet."

Oracle moved forward, a sad expression on his face.

"The time has come for me to leave.
Don't be sad and do not grieve.
Where you must travel, I can't go.
I must return to flux and flow."

Score scowled at him. "We're not going to miss you," he snapped. "You've been nothing but trouble for us from day one."

Helaine looked puzzled, though. "This is it?" she asked. "You're never coming back?"

Oracle spread his hands.

"I have done all that I can,
And you must follow others' plan.
Win or lose, I cannot tell
But I've completed all my spell.
Farewell."

Score stared at him, and Oracle's body seemed to waver, and then lose all coherence. His body simply faded, bits of him dropping off and vanishing. Like the Cheshire Cat, the last portion of him to vanish was his slightly whimsical smile. "That's it?" asked Score. "He's gone forever?" He felt a surprising loss.

He was not real, Thunder said, confused. *He was a spell made solid. He could not possibly endure. Why do you sound so sad?*

"I don't know," admitted Score. "I mean, he was a real nuisance and all. But . . . well, I guess we were kind of getting used to him."

You are certainly the most confusing humans I've ever met, Thunder snapped. *You're feeling sorry for someone you didn't much like and never trusted. And who, in fact, was not real.*

"Yeah, we're quite contrary, aren't we?" asked Pixel. He grinned. "That's just the way we are, I guess."

Score moved over to where Helaine was studying her Book of Magic. "Found something?" he asked.

"Yes," she said, showing him the page. It read: "Oracle." He glanced at the spell, which was to send a messenger made of ether to a given person.

"That's . . . that's the spell that must have created Oracle!" he realized.

"Exactly." Helaine looked grim. "Which means that either Aranak created Oracle — and I don't believe that for a second — or whoever owned this book before Aranak did. And that, presumably is Eremin. Whoever he or she is. Possibly one of the Three, do you think? There's an E on one of the thrones in the Pages. That might be Eremin."

"We're getting closer to the truth, maybe," Score said. "But is there anything in there we can use?"

Turning the page, Helaine showed him another spell. "It's a mirror spell," she explained. "It turns any magic thrown at you back on its user. It's like a magical shield."

"I like the sound of that," Pixel said, joining

them. He, too, studied the page. "We should memorize this."

Score agreed, and did so. It looked to be a very handy spell to know.

Then he felt a kind of itching in the back of his mind. It was a little like the way talking telepathically to the unicorns felt, but with a raspier edge to it. He wished he could scratch inside his skull. Then he saw the looks on Helaine's and Pixel's faces, and realized that they were feeling the same thing. "What is it?" he asked.

"Someone's trying to contact us magically," Helaine said. "I'm sure that's it."

"Not quite." Pixel's face had gone pale. "It's that magic spell," he said. "It must be Sarman! He's finished making those effigies of us, and is attempting to use them to control us! I can feel the magic trying to spread throughout my body. . . ."

Now that Pixel had said it, Score realized he felt it, too. Like tiny fires dancing down his nerves, trying to wrestle control of his body from his own mind. "Fight it!" he gasped.

"It's no good," Pixel replied, struggling. "It's too powerful."

Unicorns! Thunder cried. *To us! We must protect our friends!* He started forward.

And then there was a twisting and tearing in the air. A jagged black hole appeared and grew between the unicorns and the three humans. Thunder couldn't get past it.

"A gateway," Pixel gasped. "It's Sarman! He's creating it for us. He's going to take us to the final level."

"Fight it!" Score repeated. "We know that Sarman can't leave Jewel. If we can avoid passing through the Gateway, then he can't do anything." But even as he spoke, his legs shuddered and gave a jerky move toward the blackness. Horrified, he realized that he couldn't control his own feet. Another shuffling step brought him closer to the Gateway. Beside him, looking equally scared, Helaine and Pixel shuffled along as well.

No! Thunder howled, rearing up, his horn bright. *We shall fight this! He shall not have you!*

Even as Thunder spoke, though, the air was solid with Shadows. Whispering and laughing, they attacked the unicorns, forcing Thunder, Flame and Nova to defend themselves with their horns against the Shadows' sharp, dark claws.

The Shadows were preventing the unicorns from aiding the humans, Score realized. And his legs were dragging him step by step closer to the Gateway. Nothing he could do could win back control of his own body. He was forced to stumble along, a prisoner inside his own body.

And then he was at the Gateway. He struggled mentally as much as he could, but his feet refused to listen to his brain. He stepped into the blackness, Helaine and Pixel at his side —

— and fell through into a huge room in a dark castle. Behind him, the Gateway vanished, trapping them here. Wherever here was.

Ahead of them, seated on a throne that was carved out of an immense single diamond, sat a dark and brooding man. He stroked a black beard and smiled at them.

"I am Sarman," he purred, his ebony eyes boring into each of them in turn. "Welcome to my domain."

Score knew that he and his friends were doomed.

PART 2

CHAPTER 8

Helaine stared at Sarman as he sat forward on his throne, studying them. She could feel the magic flowing from him, and realized that he was by far the most powerful magician they had met yet. It was like an electrical current in the air, tingling her nerves and stroking her skin.

She could see in his eyes his greed, his lust for power, and his total lack of a conscience.

"Let us go," she asked proudly. She would not beg for her life.

"After going to all this trouble to bring you here?" Sarman asked, amused. "No, I think not. You're far too valuable to my plans. In fact, you're indispensable." He rose to his feet. "Isn't it nice to be important?" He strode across the room to join them.

Up close, he was even worse. Helaine could feel her skin crawl. He seemed to be radiating evil as he moved. It seethed from every pore; it clung about him like a stench. His only concern was for himself, his own desires and dreams. There was no compassion for anyone else at all.

His dark eyes zeroed in on her, and he smiled again. But it was only a movement of his mouth; there was no real humor in it. "You don't like me, do you?" he asked softly.

"You're disgusting," she replied.

He raised an eyebrow. "And you're brave," he answered. "Considering I have your bodies and souls in my power right now. But you're also stupid. Trying to anger me won't get you anywhere."

"So what will?" asked Score hopefully. "I can do a really good grovel . . . if you let me have control back over my body."

Sarman laughed. "You're almost amusing," he admitted. "If you weren't so pathetic. As to what will help you . . . *nothing* will help you. You're going to die, because it's necessary."

"Well, would you at least tell us what this is all about?" asked Pixel. "If you're going to kill us, at least don't let us die ignorant."

"What it's all about?" Sarman sighed. "It's all about *power*, of course. What else would it be?" He considered for a moment. "Very well, I may as well explain what will happen to you." He crossed to a small table beside his throne and picked up three doll-like figures. Helaine could see that these were the images he was using to control them. They were very detailed, and she saw that the lock of her hair that the Shadows had stolen was plaited into the hair of the image. "While I have these, I control you completely. But it's a strain, so I'll let you have your own legs back — for now. But behave, or I'll take command again." He snapped his fingers, and Helaine almost collapsed before she regained her feet.

She had pins and needles throughout her whole body. But it felt good to be able to control her actions once again. Her hand went instinctively toward her sword hilt, but then she stopped the motion.

"Very smart, Helaine," said Sarman. Then he smiled at her. "Yes, I know your real name. Yours, too, Matt," he added, looking at Score. "And let's not forget Shalar, shall we?" He nodded at Pixel. "Don't worry, I'm not as stupid as Aranak. I *know* your true names. You won't escape me like you escaped that idiot." He returned to his diamond throne and seated himself upon it. "Now, let me tell you a story. Feel free to sit down and listen."

Helaine did as she was bidden, sitting cross-legged on the floor. Pixel had been very smart getting Sarman to explain things to them. At the very least, it bought them time to think. And, maybe, the opportunity to strike back at Sarman. She still had the unicorn horn in her bag, and if they could focus their mind through that, then they still had a chance . . .

"A while ago, the Diadem was ruled by the Triad," Sarman explained. "Their names were Traxis, Nantor and Eremin."

At the last name, Helaine gave a start. That was the name in her Book of Magic! It had been the property of one of the Triad, then. That explained why it was filled with such useful information . . . And it explained the references on the Pages to T, N, and E. These stood for the Triad.

Sarman hadn't noticed her reaction, and continued with his tale. He was completely self-absorbed, and convinced they were no threat to him. Maybe he was right, Helaine reflected. But maybe they weren't quite as helpless as he believed.

"The Triad were idiots, of course, but *powerful* idiots. They kept the Diadem going from here, absorbed in their own petty little plots and squabbles. They didn't even notice the threat that I posed to them. I laid my plan carefully, then attacked them here. They were weakened by disagreements, and I annihilated them, stepping into their place to rule the entire Diadem."

Pixel snorted. "And then you blew it, didn't you?" he asked. "That's why everything's gone wrong."

"I did not, as you so eloquently phrased it, *blow it*," snapped Sarman, irritated. He didn't take criticism too well. "It's just that the demands made upon me were larger than I had imagined. When the Triad ruled, one of them always had to stay here on Jewel to keep the magic flowing, but the other two could travel."

"So *that's* it!" said Pixel, enjoying wounding Sarman with words. "You took over Jewel, only to discover that you're stuck here. If you leave, the magic ceases, and you're nothing."

"Watch that poisonous little tongue of yours," Sarman told him coldly. "At least, for as long as you still have it." Pixel's insults were obviously working. If Sarman got annoyed enough, he was going to start making mistakes . . . The wizard glared at them all. "Yes, I discovered that I was held captive here by my very victory. Any lesser being would have gone mad, of course, but not I. I simply began to plan for an escape that would preserve the Diadem and allow me to go wherever I pleased. A solution that never occurred to the stupid Triad." His eyes glittered as he reminisced about his own brilliance.

"Well," Score said rudely, "you can certainly praise yourself, can't you? But you're going to have to do a lot more if you expect to impress us."

"Really?" Sarman glowered at him. "Then come with me and see what my genius has created. And what you will be giving your lives to complete." He spun about and strode across the room to a large door in one wall.

Helaine considered using her sword. With his back to them, and lost in his own thoughts, she might be able to kill him from behind. But even as she thought of this, she dismissed it. He might well be planning to kill them all, but she simply couldn't bring herself to stab anyone in the back. Such a deed would be the action of a coward, not a warrior.

She saw Score looking at her, and realized that the same thought must have crossed his mind, too. He gestured to her sword, and then Sarman's back. Helaine gave a tight shake of her head. She knew it would irritate Score — he'd probably have no second thoughts about stabbing someone in the back! — but she had to be true to her own beliefs.

To her surprise, he grinned ruefully and nodded. He understood her feelings and empathized with them! Helaine realized that either he or she had changed considerably since this adventure of theirs had begun. Or maybe both of them . . .

They were all right behind Sarman when he threw open the door and said, "Behold my genius!"

Helaine was astonished at what she saw. The room beyond was totally empty save for the strange construction in the center of the wide space. It was like nothing she had ever seen before, but she could grasp what it was almost immediately.

There was a central, immense diamond, the size of a melon. Around it in spheres were dozens of glowing gems. Though nothing obvious held them in their places, the glittering jewels moved in a slow, stately path, orbiting the central diamond. There were beryls, rubies, amethysts, opals, sapphires, and gems she didn't even have names for. Every one was the size of her fist, and they had to be worth a fortune. She stood there, lost in thought and wonder as she watched the steady procession of gems.

It was a representation of the Diadem. The large diamond was Jewel, of course, and the other gems had to represent the planets, arranged in their circuits.

Beside her, she heard Pixel gasp. "It's what I've been dreaming of," he murmured. "This is it!"

"What?" Sarman turned, his face twisted with anger. "Don't be stupid, boy. You *can't* possibly have known about this. I am the only one before this moment who has ever seen it. I planned and executed this design. You're lying."

"No," Pixel said firmly. "I'm not. It's marvelous . . . But I've seen it before in my dreams."

"That simply isn't possible," Sarman said flatly. "You're just trying to annoy me, you little worm. So shut up and admire my creation for a moment, and then I'll explain further."

Helaine was intrigued. She knew that Pixel was telling the truth — he *had* seen this before in his dreams, just as she had seen the Book of Magic, and Score had heard his tune. So Sarman certainly wasn't infallible. Somehow, someone else knew about this device, and had managed to warn Pixel about it in a dream.

Pixel was entranced, seeing the real object he'd been dreaming about for so long. His eyes glittered in the gem light. Then he gestured to three of the jewels in the outermost layer. "What's wrong with them?" he asked.

Now that he'd pointed them out, Helaine saw the gems, too. There was a sapphire, a ruby, and an emerald. All three spun about the core like the other stones, but unlike them these had no inner fire. They were pretty, but somehow lifeless.

"Ah!" Sarman said, smiling in a very nasty fashion. "They are where you come in. You see, each and every jewel in this mechanism represents a single world of the Diadem. That opal near the center, for example, represents Dondar. See how brightly it burns? Well, the dull three are for Earth, Ordin and Calomir. The last three gems that will complete my magical device and free me.

"You see, it's simply an immense extension of the oldest magical trick in the book. Form, name and substance. These gems are the form of their worlds. My Shadows gathered the jewels, one from each planet of the Diadem. Then they were all named for their respective planets, and sealed with spells. All that was needed was the *substance* of their worlds.

"And that is where you three come in. To power the gems, I need to draw off the living essences of a magic-user from each planet in the Diadem. I have succeeded in all but three cases."

"Our worlds," said Pixel.

"Precisely. That is why I had my Shadows come to your worlds to force you on your journey. I needed a magic-user from Earth, Ordin and Calomir. You three were selected. I needed you to develop your powers, because the magic essence that you possess will envelop and power those final three jewels. The stronger your magic, the more powerful the final effect. That is

121

why I had Aranak begin to train you. But the fool tried to take your power for himself, thus almost thwarting my plans."

"He didn't succeed, though," Score pointed out. He was very pale, and obviously very worried. "And Garonath failed, too."

"Yes," Sarman agreed. "You really have had some amazing luck, haven't you? Well, that's all to the good, because it has finally brought you here to me. And it will give me the power I need to finish my construction. Once your souls are trapped inside those gems, my own Diadem will be completed. Then it will take over for me, stabilizing the magic of the real Diadem."

Pixel gave a gasp of understanding. "That's why the magic's all wrong, isn't it?" he asked. "Why things don't always work right. That model of the Diadem is incomplete, and it's affecting the real thing."

"Yes," agreed Sarman. "But as soon as your life forces empower the last three gemstones, then the magic will be restored. Your deaths will be doing the Diadem a great favor."

Helaine growled. "And then you'll be free to go wherever you wish, terrorizing the whole Diadem, doing whatever you want."

"In essence, yes," agreed Sarman. "Once the mechanism is fully powered, I shall rule the entire Diadem. All of the worlds will come under my sway. I shall control everything, forever. And, unlike the Triad, I won't get weak or foolish. The entire Diadem will be within my grasp, now and forever. The rule of Sarman is about to begin — with your unwilling help. I shall drain your souls into these crystals. You will be neither alive nor dead for all of eternity."

CHAPTER 9

Pixel was past the verge of panic. He realized that Sarman was absolutely serious in what he had said, and that he had every intention of doing precisely what he had threatened. He was going to steal the souls of the three of them and then take over the whole Diadem. He tried to visualize what it would mean to the other worlds when Sarman was their conqueror. Calomir would not be able to stand up against him. In fact, a lot of the inhabitants, locked in their own private forms of Virtual Reality, wouldn't even know that he had conquered their planet.

And Sarman had no concept of mercy or kindness, that was quite clear. If he ruled the Diadem, then he would ruthlessly exploit it for his own ends. Nobody and nothing would ever be safe from him.

Pixel simply couldn't allow that. It was no longer simply a matter of saving his own life and those of his friends. The stakes had just become enormous. If he, Helaine, and Score failed now, it wouldn't just be their own lives that would be ended. It would also mean the lives of every other being scattered across the worlds of the Diadem.

"Never," he said firmly. "I don't care what the cost is to me, Sarman, but I can't allow you to go through with this."

Sarman stared at him in anger for a second, then broke down into laughter. "*You* can't allow *me*?" he asked, gasping for breath. "Little worm, you have no choice in this matter. I have the power. I am in control here. The only thing that you can do now is to be absorbed."

"Not quite," Helaine growled, drawing her sword. "We can kill you first."

"Oh, please!" Sarman actually rolled his eyes and sighed. "Haven't you learned *anything* about magic?" He made a slight gesture, and Helaine froze in place. "I control you through your images, idiots."

Pixel discovered that he, too, was frozen in

place. Score gave a soft whimper as he, too, tried to move and failed. The dolls that Sarman had constructed certainly had the power that he claimed for them.

"And now for the final act, as I seize power," Sarman said smugly. He glanced around. "Shadows!" he cried. "To me!" He turned back to his three captives and shrugged. "They may only be dim-witted servants," he apologized, "but I do so want an audience as I achieve my final goal. And you three, sadly, won't be conscious to witness most of it."

There were skitterings and whispers in the air all about them, and then dark, sinewy shapes extruded themselves from the dark corners of the room. The Shadows slid and merged in the air around them, staying clear of the light from the great crystal Diadem in the center of the room.

"Right," said Sarman. "Now we can begin." He glared at the writhing Shadows. "You may burst into spontaneous applause whenever you wish. Such as *immediately*."

The Shadows somehow had enough substance to be able to clap their claws and give deep, throaty cheers, all of which Sarman ate up. He levitated himself, climbing thin air as if there were steps in it, until he was level with the three dull gemstones. A ruby, a sapphire and an emerald, Pixel saw. The gemstones that represented himself and his friends. And soon to be their tombstones.

Pixel! Score! came Helaine's voice, absolutely clearly inside his mind. Helaine was still frozen in place, her lips not moving. So how . . . Oh! Pixel had forgotten the agate that Helaine had. She was using that to speak to them without Sarman being able to overhear. But what good would it do? *Pay attention!* Helaine snapped. *Sarman's so wrapped up in gloating and anticipating his big moment of triumph that he didn't even bother to search us. We've all still got our gemstones. And the unicorn horn!*

Of course . . . In the onslaught of all his worries, Pixel had forgotten all about the horn. *Can we use it to block Sarman?* he thought back at her.

It's our only chance, Helaine answered silently. *We all have to focus our energies on it and use it to weaken his grip on us. Then we can destroy his Diadem model.*

Pixel felt a chill. *No!* he cried, *We don't touch the model. I can't explain it yet, but I know it's vitally important to leave it alone.*

Pixel, Helaine replied, *we have to destroy it, to stop Sarman.*

Hold on, Score thought. *Look, Pixel's the one

who's been dreaming about the Diadem model. I think we should trust his instincts on this one.*

Thank you, Pixel thought back at him. *I *know* it's terribly important not to harm the model.*

Helaine shrugged mentally. *Well, it doesn't make any sense to me, but if you're that certain, then I'll go along with you. So, let's all concentrate on the unicorn horn and see if we can disrupt Sarman's plans.*

Pixel concentrated, picturing in his mind the horn as it had been the last time he'd seen it. Long, spiraled and made of mother-of-pearl. Focus his energies and thoughts through it, channeling them to block Sarman's spell . . .

Oblivious to all of this, Sarman was chanting in a low voice over the three gems, activating them to receive the life forces of his next three victims. Pixel realized that Sarman had done this quite a few times before to activate the glowing gems. He must have absorbed the souls of dozens of people so far in his mad scheme to control everything. Three more victims meant nothing to him.

Then he grinned. He could start to feel life returning to his body. He managed to wiggle his toes, and then his fingers. It was working! The three of them together were starting to overcome Sarman's spell! He concentrated even harder, focusing on freeing himself . . .

And then Sarman glanced around, something having alerted him. "What?" he asked, momentarily distracted from his binding spell. "I sense . . . You three! What are you doing?"

"Defeating you!" Helaine growled, aloud this time. There was sweat on her brow, and her fingers were flexing as she gripped her sword handle. "You aren't as powerful as you think."

"That's impossible!" Sarman stared at them in shock, seeing them all starting to slowly move. "I control you! You *can't* move!" He whirled around in the air, and screamed at the closest Shadow, "You! Get their dolls from the other room and bring them to me!"

Pixel struggled to move faster, but it wasn't possible. It was like moving in slow motion. He was regaining control of his body, but too slowly. Sarman was up to something, and until they were free, they couldn't stop him.

Then the Shadow was back, the three images dangling from its claws. Sarman snatched them up, and gestured. The dolls hung in the air beside him, glowing with power. "Matt, Shalar and Helaine, I use your True Names and invoke you to obey. You are *mine*. Cease your struggling and be still!"

Pixel felt a wash of magic over him as Sarman invoked his name . . . and then it slid off him again. He continued to move, getting stronger and more mobile each second.

"It's not possible!" Sarman roared in anger. "I have control over you! You cannot be doing this!"

"Says you," growled Score. "But we *are*."

Sarman was starting to get frantic now, seeing his plans being thwarted. Whatever the three of them were doing, it was exploding his arrogance and certainty. "Then I can no longer wait," he snapped. "I shall start to drain your life forces this very second." He whirled back to his model, and started to recite a new spell.

Once again, Helaine spoke to Pixel and Score mentally. *Now!* she cried. *Focus on the unicorn horn — and use that mirror spell we all just learned. We have to turn Sarman's own magic back on himself.*

Are we strong enough to do that? asked Score. Even just mentally, his voice sounded uncertain.

We have to be, Pixel replied. *This is our only chance. Helaine's right: We must use the mirror spell. Remember what it said on the Page! *Mirror, mirror, on the wall. This is how the mighty fall.* That has to mean Sarman. Concentrate! It *will* work! It *has* to!*

Pixel followed his own advice, reciting the spell mentally, and concentrating on the horn. Even though it was still in Helaine's pack, Pixel could see it glowing brightly, even brighter than Sarman's gemstone sphere. It was working — their combined power was strong and growing stronger!

And then Sarman pounced. He whirled around in the air, and gestured at the three of them. From his fingertips, three beams of blinding, burning light shot toward them —

— only to rebound as if they had struck a shield of some kind. Sarman stared at them in horror. "No!" he screamed. "This isn't possible! I control you! You can't be doing this!"

But they could. Pixel was almost shaking with the effort, but he could feel the effect of his energies flowing through the unicorn horn.

Sarman's rays were turned back on himself. But, despite his arrogance, he wasn't entirely stupid. The rays hit some kind of a shield that he'd erected around himself. It wasn't going to be as simple to defeat him as they had hoped.

"Fools," he snarled. "I don't know what you're doing, or how you're doing it, but it will not get you anywhere. I am the master here in these halls!" He gestured again, and lights started to coalesce in the air around them like fireflies, buzzing and flitting about.

Pixel had no idea what was going on, but Helaine snapped simply, "Trouble!" He tried to move away from the lights, but he was still bogged down in Sarman's spell, even though it was weaker.

Several of the lights dived for him, spinning down from the air at his exposed skin. Pixel yelled as they touched him, burning him like acid. He couldn't escape them at all, since he couldn't run.

"Painful, isn't it?" Sarman sneered. "I can stop them whenever you wish. Just lower your shield."

"So you can steal our souls," gasped Score, batting unsuccessfully at the lights that were leaving red welts on his skin. "No thanks!"

Pixel tried to concentrate. There had to be a solution to this! But it was hard to think straight while the lights were dive-bombing him and leaving burning scars on his skin. Then he concentrated on making fire, murmuring the words to himself as he did so. Focusing, he made small balls of flame explode wherever he saw a flash of light in the air.

This worked! The acid fireflies were exploding too. But it was hard work, and he had to focus precisely right, or the lights would escape. Both Score and Helaine caught on, and they started to follow his example. Several more of the lights managed to get through to scar him before they were all destroyed.

"That won't save you," Sarman snarled. He was clearly losing his cool now. He muttered another spell, and Pixel felt as if a giant hand had grabbed hold of his chest. It squeezed hard, so that he couldn't breathe. The pain was terrible, and he gasped to try and get air into his lungs. His throat burned, and there was a wash of red haze over his mind.

"Lower your shield," Sarman purred. "And then I'll let you breathe."

Without any breath, Pixel couldn't even refuse. Instead, he tried to stifle his mounting fears. If he couldn't break free soon, he'd lose consciousness. And then Sarman could do whatever he wished, and they wouldn't be able to stop him. To have his spirit trapped for all of eternity inside one of those crystals . . . Perhaps it would be like sleeping forever, and dreaming constantly. But he didn't want to find out. He had to get free. . . .

And then he had it. While he could still focus his thoughts, he created a force field around his body, just outside of his skin. Then, summoning all of his strength, he exploded it outward.

And the pressure was gone. The invisible whatever-it-was had been thrown free by this action. He drew in a ragged breath, which hurt his throat and chest and yet felt so very good. Then he sent mental images of what he'd done to get free to both Helaine and Score, who were still gasping in the clutches of their attackers. Seconds later, red-faced and whooping, they were free, also.

We can't let this go on, he told them. *Sarman's going to win if he keeps this up. We have to stop him *now*.*

*That's easy to *think*,* Score replied. *But he's winning right now. What can we do?*

I've had an idea, Pixel said. *You two stop him from getting at me, and I'm going to try it.*

It had better be a good idea, Helaine warned him. *Because if it isn't, it's going to be your last.*

Pixel realized that she was right. Sarman had unleashed another barrage of energy spells at them. He was careful not to actually kill them — which would defeat his own plans — but he was trying to injure them or knock them out. That way, he could drain their souls into his gems.

Unless Pixel's half-baked idea worked. Pixel could feel the magic of the spell that was trying to draw their souls from their bodies. It was very powerful, and at any second it might slip past the unicorn horn disenchantment. But what surprised him the most was that it hadn't already. After all, Sarman had made his images of the three of them specifically to drain them. He had their true names, their forms, and their substance. It should have worked. Unless, somehow, one of the elements of the spell was wrong.

He'd think about that later. Right now, he had to

be as sneaky as he'd ever been. Remembering the mirror spell, he turned his mind on the soul-stealing spell that Sarman had cast. Score and Helaine were blocking the explosions that rattled the room around them, but Pixel could tell that they were getting weaker. Despite all their potential as magic-users, they were still now to this. It was draining their strength quickly, and in minutes, they would fall and Sarman would win. Unless Pixel struck first. He spun the mirror spell in with the soul spell, and then directed all of his energies at the Diadem analog.

But not at the ruby, sapphire and emerald. They were the stones associated with him, Helaine, and Score. He focused it all on the immense diamond in the center of the web. The one that represented Jewel itself. . . .

The next explosion was the closest yet, rocking him almost off his feet. He couldn't afford to let his concentration slip, but he could see Helaine stumble. Only a quick grab by Score stopped her falling. There was no more time. Sarman's next attack would defeat them.

Pixel poured all of his power into the spell: *Bind the soul into this gem,* he instructed it. *Take the diamond soul. . . .*

Sarman poised, a huge thunderbolt in his upraised hand. "This is it," he gloated. "Your energies are too drained to stop me now. It was a long fight, but —"

Sarman broke off as the powers Pixel had unleashed swirled about the room. Pixel could feel it, as he collapsed to his knees. He couldn't defend himself at all now; he was too weak, Score and Helaine were both as pale and shaking. If this didn't work, they were doomed.

Sarman blinked and shook, and his hand faltered. The glowing thunderbolt fell to the floor and dissolved into the stone. "No," he gasped, feeling the magical forces raging around him. "It isn't possible. . . ."

He had barely the time for a long, lingering scream as the magic enveloped him. Dancing lights, like summer lightning, played over his pain-wracked form. Then a glowing sphere of dazzling white light was wrenched from his body. It hovered in place for a second, while his twisted, burned corpse plunged to the floor below. Then the ball of light slid through the gemstones to the giant diamond at the heart of the Diadem model. It paused for a second, and then flowed into the immense stone.

And all the forces at work on Pixel ceased abruptly.

Chaos ruled in the room for the next few minutes.

Battered, exhausted and mentally drained, Pixel, Helaine and Score could do nothing but watch.

The Shadows all screamed, and twisted in the air more than usual. As Pixel watched, they seemed to harden, growing solid, and then, in silence, they coagulated and then shattered. Dark, smoky remains showered out of the air toward the ground. Each evaporated before they could strike the stones, however. It was a rain of Shadows, and they vanished into the light. They had only existed because of Sarman, and without him to sustain them, they were doomed.

Then the three dolls that looked like Pixel, Helaine and Score burst into greenish flames. For a second, Pixel was afraid that he would follow the example of his doll and do the same. Fire burned at every pore on his body. But then it was gone, the dolls vanishing in greenish-brown smoke, leaving no remains. Pixel felt the final bit of Sarman's control over him leave.

"It's over," Score breathed, as if he couldn't believe it.

Helaine grinned widely. "We've won!"

Score laughed in relief. "I really didn't think we were going to make it there, folks. And, for once, I'm really glad I was wrong."

Pixel's voice caught in his throat. Then he

pointed at the Diadem gems. "It's not quite over yet," he informed his friends. "Look!"

They followed his shaky finger and saw what Pixel had spotted. The central diamond was glowing brightly, and *twisting* in the air. Something was happening to it.

As they watched, three bright flakes of light flashed out of the diamond, and streaked through the air. Pixel just had time to see that both Score and Helaine were transfixed by two bolts of light before the third impacted on him.

There was a flare of brilliance that almost blinded him, and then the whole world changed, slipping away from him

What new menace was this?

CHAPTER 10

Score couldn't see anything at all for several seconds. He blinked, and rubbed at his eyes. Gradually, the afterimage of the blinding flash settled down, and he could start to make out his surroundings.

Pixel and Helaine were with him, both looking just as confused and impaired as he was. And they were no longer in the room of Sarman's castle where they had been standing. Score wasn't at all sure where they were now. The walls seemed to be made out of crystal of some kind, which distorted the way that everything looked. After a moment, he realized that it was just as if they were somehow standing inside a huge, hollowed-out diamond. For all he knew, that was exactly what they were doing.

And they were no longer alone. Seated on thrones carved from the same diamond, as if it was growing from the floor, were three strange figures. They were all adults, but their ages were hard to tell. There were two males, one on either side of the sole female. She was definitely very beautiful, but her face had such a haughty expression on it that it marred her attractiveness. The male on the left was tall and thick-set, with a heavy scowl. The one on the right was slimmer, and was almost sneering at them. All three wore long robes that were obviously very expensive. They had intricate designs stitched on them. The man on the left wore robes that were basically green. The woman's robes were a rich blue, and the final man wore red.

The same colors as he, Pixel and Helaine had seen in their dreams. And the thrones had the letters, T, N, and E carved into them. This was starting to make some kind of terrible sense to him now. Score couldn't help feeling that there was something awfully familiar about the three of them. Pixel clearly felt this even stronger. He stepped forward, pointing to the man on the right.

"I know you!" he exclaimed. "I saw an image of you in my bath on Treen!" He scowled. "I thought you were a grown-up me."

The man scowled back. "No," he replied. "I am *not* you grown-up." He seemed to find the idea distasteful. "Quite the reverse, in fact."

"What are you talking about?" asked Score. "Where are we? Who are you? What's going on?"

"Stop asking questions," the other man replied. "If you give us a chance to explain, we shall. Where are you? Well, nowhere, I suppose, is the proper reply." He waved his hand around. "This place doesn't physically exist, as you think of it. It's just a representation we conjured up. Here on Jewel, you can do *anything* at all, if you have the power and know how to use it."

"As to who we are," the woman said, her voice as icy as her face, "I would have thought that was perfectly obvious, even to you three fools. We are the Triad. I am Eremin, and these are Traxis" — that was the man on her left, who bowed his head slightly — "and Nantor."

Helaine frowned. "But you're dead," she objected.

"Yes," agreed Traxis. "And we're not enjoying it very much, I can tell you."

Score's stomach felt like it was about to do a back flip. "Then you're *ghosts*?" he demanded weakly.

"No, we're not," Traxis snapped. "We're . . . potentials."

Pixel shook his head. "You're not making any sense," he complained.

"On the contrary," Nantor answered, "we're making perfect sense. It's just that you can't understand us. You're really so poorly educated. But we didn't have very much choice in the matter."

"Really," Eremin said, rubbing her temples, "it's hurting me to try and think down to their level. Perhaps we can have someone else explain it to them."

"Not a bad idea," agreed Traxis. He snapped his fingers, and Oracle suddenly appeared beside them. "You, you idiot. It was your job to tell these three clowns what was going on. Why didn't you?"

Oracle chuckled. "Because your spell was messed up," he replied. "I couldn't do what you created me for."

Score was amazed — partly to see Oracle again, and partly because he'd finally stopped speaking in rhymes. "There must be something wrong," he complained. "You're actually starting to make sense."

"On the contrary," Oracle replied, moving closer to the three of them. "I am finally able to talk directly instead of using all those ridiculous rhymes. You have no idea how frustrating it was for me. But with Sarman's magic messing everything up, I didn't have any choice. Since you've managed to use his own magic to destroy him, though, I'm now back to being the way

I should have been. Thank you very much for that. It feels marvelous."

"We didn't summon you here so you could natter on with those brats," Eremin said snappishly. "Get on with your job, and explain things to them."

Pixel stared at her in disgust, and then turned to Oracle. "So it was the Triad who sent you to us, then? Shanara was right: You're their servant."

"That's right," Oracle answered. He chewed on his lip for a moment. "Look, this is going to be kind of complicated, so I'm going to have to explain it in stages, okay? Right, well, the Triad you've now met." He lowered his voice slightly. "What do you think of them so far?"

Score grimaced. "They're like teachers from the underworld," he muttered. "Only not quite that nice. I can see why they're not very popular in the Diadem."

"We can hear you," Traxis snapped.

"Good," Score replied. "I can think of a lot more names to call you if you'd like to hear them, too."

Eremin waved her hand impatiently. "Stop trying to bait us, child. Let Oracle get on with it. We don't have all day to waste, you know."

Oracle winked at Score and the others. "They're rather used to getting their own way, as you can probably tell."

Pixel had been puzzling things out, and he now

started to look as if he was pretty sure he had a few of the answers. Score wasn't surprised: Pixel was incredibly good at piecing things together with sometimes only the sketchiest of information to start with.

"When they worked together, their powers were unmatched," Pixel said slowly. "But they're just as bad at getting along with one another as they are at getting along with other people. They're each of them selfish and self-absorbed."

"With good reason," Nantor growled. "We're the most powerful beings in the Diadem. Of course we focus on ourselves. There's nobody to match us."

Helaine snorted. "Probably not other dead people, no," she agreed.

"And that's what started all of this," Pixel said, obviously working it out as he went along. "The three of them started to quarrel with one another, and then they stopped working together. They did manage to work out an agreement by which each of them took some time out to rule here in Jewel while the other two traveled and controlled the rest of the Diadem. But it wasn't a very harmonious arrangement.

"Sarman, meanwhile, had been growing in power. He realized that with the Triad not really getting along, their hold on Jewel and the Diadem was weakened. He knew that if he struck fast and hard enough, he could take the Triad out and seize control of the Diadem himself. So he laid his plans and then struck."

"But we were too smart for him," Traxis added.

"Then how come you're dead?" sneered Score.

"A delaying tactic," replied Eremin.

"Some tactic," muttered Pixel.

"No," Oracle explained, not bothering to try and smother the grin on his face. He might be a servant of the Triad, but he clearly didn't have much love for them, and was enjoying it whenever Score or one of the others managed a sly reply. "It did work, in a peculiar way. When Sarman struck, these three couldn't get together properly to form a full defense against his powers. They were too busy squabbling with each other. So they were forced to evolve a rather unique plan. Sarman had them under assault here on Jewel, and there was no way they could possibly escape without him knowing about it. But they were able to discover his plans, and knew that he was going to create his Diadem analog — those spinning jewels that you saw. In fact, he was planning to use the life forces of the Triad to animate the diamond that stands for Jewel."

Pixel snapped his finger. "And when we reversed his spell, and made him absorb his own life force and not ours, naturally it went to the diamond — and displaced the life forces of the Triad!"

So *that* was what the flashes of light they had seen had been!

"Correct," agreed Oracle.

"But they were just life forces, and not living people," said Pixel. "They're not quite back to life yet. They're potential people right now, not quite properly alive." He pointed at the Triad, who were looking bored with this explanation. "They're back, but not all the way. There's still more that needs to be done."

"Go on," encouraged Oracle, looking very proud of Pixel. "You're absolutely right so far."

"They foresaw what Sarman was going to do, and they planned for it," continued Pixel, his face getting flushed as he knew he was getting closer to the truth. "His scheme is actually a rather brilliant one. Using the gemstones as an analog to the Diadem to keep the magic in place is quite clever, and something *they* never thought about."

"Because we didn't *need* to," Eremin snapped nastily. "We upheld the Diadem by our own powers. If we'd had to, I'm sure we'd have thought of the same thing."

"Of course you would," muttered Oracle sarcastically. "They're so arrogant, aren't they?"

"They're the most unlikable people I've ever met in my life," Helaine admitted. "And, considering some of my father's friends and the . . . man he wanted me to marry, that's saying something."

"Yeah," agreed Score. "I think they're even worse in their way than my dad."

"Oh, get on with it," grumbled Nantor. "We didn't bring you back so that you could insult us, Oracle. Do what you're created for, or we'll uncreate you and explain everything ourselves."

"If you could explain things yourselves, you wouldn't have bothered bringing me back," Oracle said calmly. Then he turned back to Score and the others. "They may have created me, but they can't make me *like* them," he confessed. "Go on, Pixel."

"They couldn't escape from Jewel without being detected," Pixel said. "And once they were off Jewel, their powers would diminish. We know that the farther you get from Jewel, the weaker the magic gets. So if Sarman could beat them here, he'd be able to trace and murder them anywhere they tried to hide.

"So they decided they had to die in order to live. They had to let Sarman kill them — but to do it their way. Their life forces would be used to power his Diadem model, and then they knew he'd go looking for a magic-user from every world of the Diadem to complete his plan. Because Earth, Ordin, and Calomir are the farthest worlds out on the Rim, those would be the last places he'd look. They also realized that his search would take years — about twelve in all. So they had the time to do what was needed.

"They had to make the three of us their secret weapons.

"They did this quite sneakily, I have to admit. Knowing where and when Sarman would strike on our worlds, they had to arrange for the three of us to be there at the right time and the right place to be taken. That was part of your job, right, Oracle?"

"Yes," he agreed. "I had to get you to the Gateways, where you would be met by the Beastials. I also had to make sure you were in such sticky predicaments that you'd accompany the Beastials without a second thought. I'm sorry that I had to betray you all to do this, but I honestly didn't have any other choice. I had to provoke you into taking that leap."

Score sighed. "It's okay, Oracle," he said. "It wasn't your fault. You were only doing what you had to do. I guess I don't feel so bad about you now."

"Thank you." Oracle shrugged. "That was when I discovered that the magic that had created me had gone wrong, and been affected by Sarman's bungling his magical transfer. I wasn't able to speak properly, and there was a compulsion on me not to tell the direct truth. So I was reduced to warning you in rhymes that couldn't ever say exactly what I wanted them to.

Instead, you kept getting riddles from me." He spread his hands helplessly. "I did my best."

"And it wasn't good enough," snapped Eremin. "They were suspicious of you, and didn't listen to you."

"And you didn't tell them any of the important stuff," grumbled Nantor. "Luckily, we had a backup plan in case you fouled up. Which you did."

"Backup plan." Oracle rolled his eyes and tried not to laugh. "All those cryptic messages that they couldn't understand. The ones on the rocks and everything."

Pixel frowned. "They were left for us by the Triad? We really didn't understand most of them at the time."

"That's because they're not very good at explaining anything," Oracle answered. "They thought the messages were all absolutely obvious. Just like the Pages they scattered."

Eremin sniffed. "It's not our fault those idiots were too stupid to understand what we were telling them," she said. "It's all quite clear if you have half a brain."

"So everything has been coming from these three lunatics?" asked Score with a sigh. "I'm starting to see why it was so hard to figure out. They're so arrogant, it never occurred to them that other people might not get it."

"We couldn't make the meaning too obvious," Traxis snapped. "We knew the Pages would be found by other wizards, who would want to know what they said. So we had to make them a little difficult to follow. But, honestly, we thought the three of you would have no problem in figuring them out."

"Well, you were wrong," Pixel answered. "It took us far too long to work out most of what they say. And some of it we still don't get. But we're getting there."

"And we were relying on *them*?" Eremin asked, appalled. "Frankly, I'm astonished they made it this far. They seem to be so dull-witted."

"Okay, knock it off with the insults," Score said, annoyed. "Let me get something straight here. You *knew* all of this was going to happen? So you knew we'd make it this far, and that we were in no real danger all along?"

"Of course not." Traxis sighed, and glared at Oracle. "You'd better explain it; you're almost as dumb as they are."

"I'd rather be on their level than yours, thank you very much," Oracle answered. Then he turned back to Score. "They can't predict *certainties*," he explained. "Only *potentialities*. They could know, for example, that you'd have to enter Treen near Aranak's tower, and that Sarman would use Aranak to try and gauge your powers. That's why they hid the Page there, and set the clues round about the tower. You were bound to stumble on them. But they couldn't guarantee you'd survive. They could only hope that you would."

"And with the aid of Oracle and the clues and Pages, you should have figured out what was going on before you got here," added Nantor. "That way, we could have done without all of these tedious explanations and gotten right to the point of this meeting."

Helaine glared at him, and then turned back to Oracle. "I think we've got most of the story now," she said. "At least, it makes some sense. But there are still two things I don't understand. Maybe you can clear them up, Pixel. You seem to have figured it out pretty well so far."

"I'll try," Pixel promised, looking pleased at her compliments. Score sighed. Pixel was definitely developing a serious crush on Helaine. Anyone could seen it — except, apparently, Helaine.

"First, why *us*?" Helaine asked. "Is it just that we happened to be potential magicians in the right place at the right time? And, second, what do they want with us? Why are we here?"

Pixel looked worried. "Well," he said slowly, "the answer to both questions is really the same, if I'm right. We were picked because only the three of us would do. The Triad prepared us specifically. That's why Score's mother had one of the Pages. And why we had those weird dreams. They were getting us ready."

Oracle nodded. "In fact, they prepared for this mission before you were born. Their plan began when the three of you did."

"As to what they want of us . . ." Pixel looked very disturbed now. "They want our lives." He gestured at the Triad. "As Oracle said, they're potentialities right now. Life forces, but not living beings."

Score went white with shock. "You mean . . . they want to take over our bodies? Come back to life again in *us*?"

"No," Pixel said slowly. "It's worse than that." He stared at Nantor. "He gave me the final clue when he said that he wasn't me grown-up. 'Quite the reverse, in fact,' was his reply." Pixel shook his head. "We don't really exist. They're not trying to take us over. They *are* us."

CHAPTER 11

Helaine stared at Eremin, confused and worried. "What do you mean?" she demanded. "Of course we exist. And we're certainly not *them*."

Oracle cleared his throat, embarrassed. "Well, not *technically*, maybe. But Pixel's right."

White-faced, Pixel continued with his thoughts. "Remember, Oracle told us that the Triad couldn't escape from Jewel without Sarman spotting them and coming after them? Well, there *was* one way out for them. You see, it would be their magical abilities that Sarman would hunt down. So the Triad divested themselves of that, leaving their magical potential here on Jewel. And since Sarman would look for adults, they hid themselves as babies. They formed themselves new bodies inside each of our mothers, and imbued these bodies — our bodies — with their own spirits. All they left on Jewel was their magical potential and their life forces. It was enough to make Sarman think they were still here. And enough for them to complete their plans.

"So when Sarman attacked, he was certain he'd destroyed the Triad and imprisoned their life forces inside his great diamond that is the heart of his Diadem analog. But, in fact, the Triad lived on — as the three of us." He gestured at the three figures on the thrones. "Like the fifth Page said: three equals three. The three of them equal the three of us. They're like recordings of people right now. Not fully alive and not fully dead. But they want to become alive again."

Eremin leaned forward, staring down at Helaine with disgust. "Much as it pains me to admit it, you're *me*."

Traxis smiled nastily at Score. "And you're me."

"Guess who you are?" Nantor asked Pixel.

Helaine was shocked and, even more, appalled. "That can't be true," she protested. "I'm not you. I'm *me*."

"You naturally think that," Eremin told her haughtily. "But that's because you don't know any better. You possess all of my being, except the fullness of my magic and the consciousness of my memories. And those you will regain when we merge. I will become whole again. You were me once, and will be me once again when what is left of me merges with all of you."

A shudder passed through Helaine at the thought. "No," she said firmly. "I'm *myself*. I'm not you. And I don't want to become you."

A slight frown creased Eremin's forehead. "Don't be ridiculous," she snapped. "You *are* me. And as soon as I take over your body, you'll know it."

Helaine shook her head. "You just don't get it, do you?" she asked. "I'm *not* you." She waved her hand at Eremin. "Sitting there, talking like I'm *nothing*, just a thing to play with. Like I have no rights, no personality. Just some toy for you to use and then throw away. Well, that's not true."

Eremin sighed. "How very tedious. Of course it's true. You are *me*. The essence of what I am. You simply refuse to accept it. But you will, when I return to take possession of you again."

Helaine glanced at Score and Pixel. She could see from the set expressions on their faces that they understood her — and, more importantly, that they agreed with her. "No," she said. "Maybe we were *supposed* to be you. But we aren't. You're arrogant, cold, selfish, and self-absorbed. And that's not us. Okay, maybe I have a tendency toward arrogance, but it's not developed. I can fight it. And, unlike you, I *care* about people. You can't even get along with your partners there. Pixel, Score and I are *friends*. We're different from you, however you planned it."

"You're mistaking a few minor points for real differences," Traxis said. "We always knew that part of the reason why we were defeated and destroyed by Sarman was because we couldn't get along. So we stressed over and over to you that you had to get along. It doesn't have to continue now that you've won the battle for us."

Score shook his head. "You just don't get it, do you?" he commented, amazed. "We didn't win any battle for *you*. We won it for *us*. And I don't want to give up being their friend." He looked haunted for a moment. "I've never really had any friends before. I've always been a loner. I never thought I could ever trust anyone. That everybody else was always interested in me only for what they could get out of me. Well, Helaine and Pixel proved me wrong. They're good friends, and I like it this way. I want that to remain."

"Me too," agreed Pixel. "On my world, all of my friends were just virtual friends. I never even knew if they were real. Well, Helaine and Score *are* real. They've both risked their lives for me, and I've done the same for them. I'm not going to give it up."

"So," Helaine finished, feeling a warm glow within

her towards the two boys, "the short, simple message is: Get lost. We're *not* you, and we have no intentions of ever becoming you." She stared at them in disgust. "You're dead, and, frankly, I think Sarman did the universe a favor by killing you. You're poisonous, and we don't ever need you back."

Fremin looked at Traxis and Nantor in astonishment. "They think they have a *choice*," she exclaimed. "What wretched little worms they are."

"Fortunately," Nantor said, smirking, "we don't need your permission. While we didn't exactly expect you to oppose our plan, neither did we leave its fulfillment entirely to chance. Once we met you again, everything was set into motion. You have no option."

Oracle sighed. "I'm sorry," he told Helaine, Score, and Pixel. "But they're right. This whole thing was their idea. This is, if you like, an ambush. They have you in the power of their spell, and there's nothing I can do to help you. I wish I could, because I like the three of you. And I don't like *them*. But in a few minutes, you will become them. There's no way of stopping this."

Helaine's heart sank. It was one thing to say what she had — and she meant it — but if Oracle and the Triad were telling the truth, then she and her friends were doomed. She looked again at Eremin. She could see herself inside there, somewhere. The same basic looks, yes, and some of the same characteristics. Eremin's arrogance might well have been her own once, if she'd continued her life the way she had been living it. When she'd first met Score and Pixel, she *had* been terribly arrogant. She'd been a warrior and a noblewoman, and she *knew* she was better than them.

Only, they had forced her to change her mind. She had come to realize that she wasn't any better than them. That they were, in their own ways, just as good as she was. She'd come to respect and like them. Something that Eremin had never done with another human being. She had joined up with Traxis and Nantor only for convenience because they were stronger together. Eremin didn't *like* her colleagues at all. That was a world of difference between her and Helaine.

And Helaine didn't want to lose any of this. Even with all the possibilities that might come from being Eremin, she knew it would be at the expense of what made her truly *her*. If Eremin took over her body, she'd become *Eremin*, not *Helaine*. And that must not happen.

Not simply because she'd no longer exist, but because Eremin would then exist in her place. And, as Helaine looked into the glassy eyes of the wizard, she knew that unleashing Eremin on the Diadem again would be a terrible disaster. She had learned *noth-*

ing from what she had gone through. She had not changed at all. She would still be the tyrant that everyone hated. Helaine felt sick to think that there was, within her, the possibility that she, too, might have become a similar tyrant if she hadn't changed. But she knew that it was true. Deep inside her, there was an Eremin locked in her soul. Only Helaine had never allowed that inner Eremin to emerge. And she never would.

Except that Eremin herself was planning on taking over her body and becoming that despicable individual once again.

Helaine held her head high. "I'd sooner die than become you," she announced.

"Likewise," agreed Score and Pixel beside her.

Traxis snorted. "As if you have any say in the matter," he sneered. "You are us, and we shall now reclaim our own." He nodded to his two companions, and they all three acted in unison.

Helaine had thought that she was prepared for any kind of magical onslaught. They still had their crystals, and the unicorn horn. Together she, Score and Pixel could stand up against anything. Or so she thought.

The Triad were singing. Their voices melded together beautifully. The song they began was deeply sorrowful, and yet with a core of hope to it. The music of it touched Helaine's mind, slipping inside her thoughts, stirring her feelings. . . .

"It's the tune," gasped Score. "The one from my dreams! That's how they're going to do it — through the music!"

It was getting harder for Helaine to think, but the truth of what he was saying broke through to her. Somehow it *was* the music that was affecting her. It was a tune that was buried deep within her, and it was struggling to get free. She could tell that this was how Eremin was reclaiming her. Through the music . . .

But what could they do about it? The Triad continued to sing, and she was growing weaker and weaker. It was getting too hard to fight off. But if she didn't, then the Triad would win. She'd become Eremin, loosing that tyrant on the Diadem again.

No! She couldn't allow that to happen! She had to fight it! She *had* to!

But how?

There was only one possible solution that she could think of: the unicorn horn. It had the power to block magic. She had to *focus*. And she needed help. Trying to fight off the effects of the song, she sent a mental call to both Score and Pixel: *Help me!* She could never break free of this terrible song using only her own strength. She had to have their help.

And she felt it flowing into her from them. They had been telling the truth when they had said they were friends, and worked together. They *had* learned, and they *had* changed. They were no longer people who could turn out to be the tyrants of the Triad.

She concentrated on the horn, picturing it in her mind, feeling it grow in power. Her consciousness was sinking downward still, though. She could feel the fringes of Eremin's dreadful, cold mind touching hers. The arrogant woman was starting to take control of Helaine's mind and soul. If the song wasn't disrupted soon, Helaine would be as good as dead. Worse: She'd become a person she absolutely loathed.

It had to work! It had to! They didn't have any other chance now. Focus . . . focus . . .

And then it leaped into bright, pulsing light. The glow from the horn penetrated the whole room, and, along with it, a single, crystal-clear musical note.

The song that the Triad had been singing was shattered by the purity of that single, lingering tone.

Abruptly, the pressure was gone from within Helaine's head. She staggered forward, free once again to think. Eremin's mind had vanished, returned to the icy body on the throne. From the gasps of relief Pixel and Score gave, she knew that they were free, too.

Wondering what the Triad would do next, Helaine stared at the three figures on the thrones.

They were sitting absolutely rigidly, no sign of any activity at all. And, beside her, Oracle was also frozen in place, a faint smile on his face. Helaine stared from one to the other, not understanding.

Pixel grinned. "We stopped their plan," he explained. "The unicorn horn broke up their song and spell. Their transfer of themselves into our bodies didn't happen, so now they're stuck in some kind of limbo. If you like, the recording's ground to a halt."

"What about Oracle?" asked Score. "You know, I have to admit he's grown on me, now that he's making sense. And he seems to dislike the Triad as much as we do."

"They created him," Pixel answered thoughtfully. "I guess with them out of action, he is, too."

"Does he have to be?" asked Helaine. "I mean, I know he's not real, as such. But he *seems* real to me. Leaving him like this is kind of like letting him die."

Pixel thought it over. "Well, if *we* are the Triad — at least in embryo — then we should be able to animate him, too. Let's use your agate and try and contact him mentally. If there's anything there, maybe we can bring him back to life."

"Right." Helaine fished out her agate, and held it in her palm, facing the frozen Oracle. "Together, now . . ." She reached out with her mind, and felt *something* there. It was like seeing a fish frozen inside a block of ice. "He's there," she said. "But trapped."

"Focus on freeing him," Pixel ordered.

Helaine nodded, and together they bent their wills toward that end. For a moment, nothing seemed to happen. And then Oracle's smile became wider, and he moved slightly.

"Thank you," he said, obviously amazed. He flexed his fingers and raised his eyebrows. "You've brought me back again. Though I'm not sure why. I thought you didn't particularly like me."

"You've improved a lot since you stopped all that rhyming," Score told him with a grin. "And you were on our side."

Oracle shrugged. "That was why I was created. I'm just doing my job." He turned to regard the Triad. "Well, whatever you've done to them seems to have been very effective. They're completely frozen and inert. What do you aim to do with them now?"

"Do?" Helaine shook her head, puzzled. "We weren't planning on doing anything with them. Let them stay like that. The Diadem is better off without them." She looked around at the crystal walls. "And I'll be happy if we can figure out how to get out of here."

"That's easy enough," Oracle answered. "This

place doesn't physically exist. You're still really inside Sarman's castle. All of this is just an illusion they cooked up. So if you just focus on seeing reality, you'll get back."

Pixel gave him a smile. "See? You're already making yourself pretty useful. Bringing you back was definitely a good idea." He looked at Helaine and Score. "Well, I guess we'd better concentrate."

Helaine nodded. She ordered her mind to stop seeing the illusion about her and to instead show what was actually there. The walls of crystal shimmered and then vanished, to be replaced by the stone walls and floors of the castle. They were still standing beside the huge Diadem analog, which was spinning slowly on its axis.

Suspended in the air in front of them were three frozen chips of light.

"So that's what is really going on," Helaine said to Oracle. "Hey, how much do you know? And how much can you help us with?"

Oracle shrugged. "I know everything that the Triad programmed into me," he replied. "And I'll be more than happy to help you in any way I can."

"Terrific." Helaine looked around the room in disgust. "I, for one, have had more than enough of this place. Can you tell us how to open a Gateway back to

Dondar? I know Flame and the others are going to be frantic with worry about us."

"Opening a Gateway should be simple enough, considering your powers," Oracle replied. "But I don't think you've really realized your predicament. You can't leave Jewel, you know. You're stuck here now."

CHAPTER 12

Oracle's statement was like a physical blow. Pixel stared at him, not comprehending. "Why can't we leave?" he demanded. "We've defeated Sarman and stopped the Triad . . ." His voice trailed off as he suddenly realized the point of that. "Of course!" he gasped. "We *have* defeated Sarman and the Triad." His two friends stared at him, not understanding. He gestured around him. "This is all kept in place by magic," he explained. "The whole Diadem is. And the magic is sustained by the power that rules Jewel. It used to be the Triad, until Sarman destroyed them. And it used to be Sarman — only we destroyed him."

Helaine went pale as the meaning sunk in. "In other words . . . *we* now rule the Diadem. . . ."

"Got it in one," Oracle said cheerily. "Ultimate power is yours. There's nobody and nothing on the Diadem now that can stop you. How does that feel?"

Pixel considered the concept: The three of them were now the most powerful beings in the entire Diadem. Whatever they wanted, they could have. Nobody and nothing could stop them

"It's appalling," he finally said. "I mean — *ultimate power*? Me? I can't even make up my mind what I want for breakfast, let alone how to run the Diadem. I'd make the world's worst ruler."

"Next-to-worst," said Score, just as glumly. "I mean, just look at me. I'm a street kid at heart. I lie, steal and swindle. Exactly the wrong sort of person to put in charge of anything." He glanced at Helaine. "At least you'd probably do all right," he commented. "You're from a ruling family, after all. You've probably got the inside track on this ruling the universe stuff."

"No," Helaine shook her head firmly. "You know, when I saw Eremin, I saw myself as I might be. Totally self-absorbed, absolutely convinced of my own right, and totally arrogant. All of those failings are inside me right now. I think that if I did become ruler of the Diadem, then I'd turn into Eremin, sooner or later."

Pixel nodded. "I think you're right. This kind of power shouldn't be held by any human being. Nobody could handle it without getting corrupted by it."

"Well," said Oracle, "that's all fine and dandy, and I admire your wisdom in this matter. The problem is that it doesn't matter what you *want*. You're stuck with the power anyway. If you try and leave here now, the magic will be uncontrolled. It would cause chaos across the entire Diadem. Worlds could be destroyed; people could die; cockroaches could conquer the universe. That sort of thing. So, like it or not, you're stuck with this power."

Pixel's heart fell like a lead weight. Oracle was right: They were stuck here, whether they wanted to be in charge or not . . .

Or were they?

"Wait a minute," he said excitedly. "The Diadem analog!"

"What about it?" asked Score.

"Sarman was building it to handle the magic," Pixel answered. "It's almost completed. If we can finish it off, then maybe it can take over the control of the magic and free us."

Helaine grinned widely, and then bent forward and kissed his cheek. "You're a genius, Pixel!"

Blushing, he couldn't meet her gaze. Or Score's,

either; the other boy was clearly amused by Pixel's embarrassment. "Well, *if* it works," he said.

Oracle studied the analog carefully, rubbing his chin and walking around it. "This is quite ingenious," he admitted. "Sarman was quite the thinker. You know, you may be right. If you can get this up and running properly, then it *could* take over the flow of magic. However, it's not going to be easy." He gestured at the three dark crystals. "For one thing, you're going to have to power up these three. And that means the life forces of three people associated with these worlds. So . . . who do you plan on killing?"

That wiped the grin off Pixel's face. "Nobody!" he protested. "We couldn't do that."

"So," Score said, sighing deeply, "that fixes that brilliant idea. Unless we kill three people and steal their life forces, the whole thing won't work."

Helaine frowned. "Not necessarily," she said slowly. She pointed at the three frozen chips of light in the air. "What about the Triad? All they are now are frozen life forces. In effect, just what we need. And they're each associated with one of us . . ."

"Brilliant!" Pixel exclaimed happily. "Of course they are! *You're* the genius, not me."

To his surprise, Helaine went slightly red, and looked rather pleased.

Pixel turned back to Oracle. "Okay, suppose we do that — switch the Triad into those three gems. Will that be enough to make this work?"

Oracle considered the matter for a moment. "Almost," he finally decided. "In a way, the Triad *are* you, so that would fulfill the requirement of someone from those worlds powering the three gems. But you'd have to seal them in with portions of your magic. You'll have to make an imprint of yourselves, too. And that would mean leaving some of your power behind. If it works, you won't be as powerful magicians as you are now."

"That's fine by me," Pixel replied. "I never asked to be a magician in the first place. I'll be happy to go back to being normal again."

"Normal for you," Oracle answered, "*is* being a magic-user. But you won't lose that much. You'll just drop down to a level where you can live comfortably anywhere in the Diadem that you choose. You could even go home again if you want to."

Pixel hadn't really thought about that. "Home?" He cast his mind back over only a few days, and found it was very difficult to remember home. It was, after all, just a box where he'd lived in Virtual Reality. And since then, he'd discovered real reality.

And it was much better.

Would he miss his parents? Would they miss

him? He didn't know. But he knew that, right now, that wasn't home.

"I think I'd sooner go back to Dondar," he replied. "I kind of like the unicorns there."

"Me too," agreed Helaine. "If I went back home, I'd be a nobody again, forced to marry some idiot Lord because of power politics. I'd sooner run free with the unicorns, thank you very much. And pick who I want to marry, when the time comes." Pixel noticed she gave him a quick, embarrassed look. Maybe she was starting to feel something for him, after all?

"And as for me," Score snorted, "what do I have to go back to? Sure, New York's the greatest city on Earth. But I'm not confined to Earth now, am I? I'd like to travel, see the worlds . . . and irritate Thunder some more."

"Well," Oracle said, "it sounds like the three of you know your own minds pretty well. Perhaps we'd better get on with it and see if this idea of yours actually will work." He studied the spinning gems again. "You'll have to focus your minds and send the Triad into the right gems. Then picture your magic as a kind of cloak about you. Picture yourselves taking that cloak off and casting it over the appropriate gem. Then seal it there."

Pixel nodded. His gem was the ruby, of course. Score's was the emerald and Helaine's was the sapphire. They moved to be able to see their gems. Concentrating, he reached out with his power and fixed on the frozen chip of light that was Nantor's life force. He pictured it moving toward the ruby, and then fusing with it. As he focused, he saw all three lights fly through the air toward the waiting gemstones. Then he could feel Nantor's light enter the ruby. Quickly, he pictured his magic as a cloak about him, as Oracle had said. Mentally, he then removed that cloak and threw it over the ruby.

Instantly, the ruby flared into bright, pulsing light. Beside it the sapphire and the emerald did the same.

Pixel felt a little light-headed as he realized that it had worked. Their plan had actually succeeded! He could feel his own power levels were now lower than they had been, but, as Oracle had predicted, he still had magic about him. He was glad that he wasn't quite as powerful now. Too much power seemed to corrupt anyone who had it. It was better not to tempt himself.

"So that's it?" asked Score. "It's all done and we can go now?"

"Almost." Oracle turned to Helaine. "The analog is working, and it will regulate the magic of the Diadem, which is now healed. Spells will work as they should again. However, it is always possible that somebody might be able to get here and do some damage to the model. You need to seal it off. And that means the unicorn horn."

Obviously with reluctance, Helaine took the horn from her bag. "Do we have to?" she asked. "This is really useful."

"I think he's right," Pixel said. "We do have to stop anyone messing with this again. And the horn is the best way of ensuring it."

With a sigh, Helaine handed Pixel the horn. "I guess you're right," she agreed. "But it's hard to part with it."

"I understand." Pixel took the horn, and turned back to the doorway to the analog room with it. Then he frowned as he noticed something. "There's a crack in this," he commented, holding the horn to show it. It was very thin, but ran for about six inches from the base of the horn. "Will it be all right?"

Oracle shrugged. "There's no way to be certain. It might hold up forever. Or it might crack and break apart. You'll only know by trying."

"I guess we *have* been overusing it a bit," Score said. "Fingers crossed, it'll hold."

What else could they hope? Pixel concentrated, and felt his friends join with him again. The unicorn horn began to glow, as it set up a magical dampening field around the approach to the Diadem model. "Nobody using magic can enter that room as long as the horn's intact," Pixel announced with certainty. "And that includes us. And nobody who doesn't use magic can reach Jewel anyway. That's as safe as we can make things."

"You've all done very well," Oracle informed them. He smiled. "I'm proud to know you all. Now, if you ever need me again, you know how to call me. As soon as you return to Dondar, I'll be off."

"Off where?" asked Pixel curiously. "Where do you vanish to when you're not needed?"

Oracle shook his head. "Maybe I'll tell you one day," he answered evasively. "But not now. Right, all of you, pay attention. To create a Gateway, you have to pierce the continuum between here and Dondar. Helaine, the spell you'll need is in your book, near the back. I'm sure you can find it."

Helaine took out her Book of Magic. She opened it, and then gave a small gasp of surprise. Pixel looked over her shoulder, and grinned. The bookplate now read: *Property of Helaine.*

"Well, that's certainly right," he said.

Helaine looked amused as she flicked through the pages. With conviction, she stopped on one handwritten page. "This is it," she said. "Let's do it."

Together, they concentrated, and recited the words of the spell. There was a moment of apprehension for Pixel as he wondered if they had done it right. He could feel that his powers were at a lesser level than they had been. Maybe they no longer had enough strength for this?

And then the familiar slash of pure blackness appeared in the air in front of them. He grinned with relief. "Time to go." He waved a hand at Oracle. "See you." Then he stepped through the blackness.

And into Garonath's castle.

It looked just as it had when they had left it earlier. Except that there were no unicorns here now.

Pixel couldn't help feeling disappointed. "Where's Thunder and the others?" he asked. "I sort of expected them to be waiting here."

"Me too," agreed Helaine. She looked even more disturbed than Pixel. "I'll just see if I can find them," she added, taking out her agate. She focused her attention on it, and then gave a cry, wrenching free of her spell.

"That was Flame!" she exclaimed. "She's in really serious trouble. And so are all of the other unicorns. We have to go to their help immediately."

Score signed. "We've just finished battling for our lives," he complained. "You think we'd get *some* rest." Helaine threw him a filthy look. "Okay," he agreed, throwing up his hands in surrender. "I'm with you. Let's get moving, then."

"Thunder's fighting for his life right now," Helaine said grimly. "I just hope we're in time. . . ."

ABOUT THE AUTHOR

JOHN PEEL is the author of numerous best-selling novels for young adults, including installments in the Star Trek, Are You Afraid of the Dark?, and Where in the World Is Carmen Sandiego? series. He is also the author of many acclaimed novels of science fiction, horror, and suspense.

Mr. Peel currently lives on the outer rim of the Diadem, on the planet popularly known as Earth.

CAN **YOU** BREAK THE CODE ON DONDAR?

#3: Book of Magic
John Peel

The Magic Is Theirs. The Power Is Yours.
Enter A New Dimension....

Score, Renald, and Pixel are about to enter the core of the Diadem and
discover they are not the three teenagers they thought they were. Will
their magical powers be enough as they face the ultimate challenge —
their creator? Will they finally unlock their true identity? And if they
do, who will rule the Diadem throne?

DIA3297